# TOGO

# DOG DIARIES

# DOG DIARIES

## TOGO

BY KATE KLIMO • ILLUSTRATED BY TIM JESSELL

RANDOM HOUSE 🏠 NEW YORK

The author and editor would like to thank Laura Samuelson, director, Carrie M. McLain Memorial Museum, Nome, Alaska, for her assistance in the preparation of this book.

Text copyright © 2014 by Kate Klimo
Cover art and interior illustrations copyright © 2014 by Tim Jessell
Photographs courtesy of Carrie M. McLain Memorial Museum/Alaskastock.com, pp. 161, 163; Underwood & Underwood/Corbis, p. 162

All rights reserved. Published in the United States by Random House Children's Books, a division of Random House LLC, a Penguin Random House Company, New York.

Random House and the colophon are registered trademarks of Random House LLC.

Visit us on the Web! randomhouse.com/kids

Educators and librarians, for a variety of teaching tools, visit us at RHTeachersLibrarians.com

*Library of Congress Cataloging-in-Publication Data*
Klimo, Kate.
Togo / Kate Klimo ; illustrated by Tim Jessell. — First edition.
pages cm. — (Dog diaries ; #4)
Summary: "Sled dog Togo—the true hero of the 1925 Serum Run—narrates the story of his life working with musher Leonhard Seppala." —Provided by publisher.
Includes bibliographical references.
ISBN 978-0-385-37335-7 (trade) — ISBN 978-0-385-37336-4 (lib. bdg.) — ISBN 978-0-385-37337-1 (ebook)
1. Togo (Dog)—Juvenile fiction. 2. Siberian Husky—Juvenile fiction. [1. Togo (Dog)—Fiction. 2. Siberian Husky—Fiction. 3. Sled dogs—Fiction. 4. Dogs—Fiction. 5. Seppala, Leonard, 1877–1967—Fiction. 6. Diphtheria—Alaska—Fiction. 7. Alaska—History—1867–1959—Fiction.] I. Jessell, Tim, illustrator. II. Title.
PZ10.3.K686Tog 2013 [Fic]—dc23 2013010754

Printed in the United States of America

10 9 8 7 6 5 4 3 2 1

First Edition

In memory of Leonhard Seppala, a dog's man

—K.K.


To the tireless, dedicated, and dutiful sled dog

—T.J.

## CONTENTS

## All Alaska Sweepstakes

Candle
Gold Run
Telephone • Haven
Council • Boston
Timber
Nome • Solomon • Topkok
Port Safety
Cape Nome

Nome

Nenana • Fairbanks

# ALASKA

Anchorage

Seward

Bering Sea

## 1925 Serum Run

Gulf of Alaska

## Showtime for Togo

There were twenty of us huskies hitched to the sled, lined up two by two, with me in the lead and Fritz as my double lead. Sepp made the rounds like he always did before a run. He checked the gang line for wear. Then he checked the harnesses and the necklines and the tug lines. I shot him a look when he came to me. *Sepp, old man, you know as well as I do that this rig's good as new.*

Why wouldn't it have been? We hadn't done an honest day's work for over a month, not since Sepp had dragged us onto that stinking tub in Nome and shipped us down to the States. The Lower Forty-Eight, we called them in Alaska, the place where sled dogs were, in those days, about as common as harbor seals.

In Alaska in the 1920s, dogsleds were the only dependable way folks could get from one place to another in all that snow and ice. Horses and mules froze their long, skinny legs off. Airplanes couldn't carry enough fuel. Trains got buried in drifts of snow. And there were no automobiles up there in those days because there were no roads. Strange as it sounds, most folks in the States had never seen a dog team pulling a sled. And that's why we were taking this tour. To show everybody what a team of dogs and their musher could do—not that they'd ever really understand our world.

Our musher's name was Leonhard Seppala (LEH-nerd SEP-luh), but most folks just called

2

him Sepp. Sepp was what you might call a Dog Man. He knew dogs; he loved dogs. Heck, he even spoke Dog. Some of these dogs would have run for any musher. But not me. I ran for Sepp, because I was Sepp's and Sepp was mine. I loved that little Norseman.

Our days of racing and delivering freight and passengers were over. Lately, all we did was travel by train from town to town, putting on shows. Everywhere we went, a marching band would strike up a tune as we pulled our sled down the center of yet another Main Street. If there wasn't any snow— and the Lower Forty-Eight had a shameful short- age of the stuff—we pulled Sepp in a wooden cart with wheels. Folks would line up along the way to greet us. In one town, they said we got a bigger crowd than Calvin Coolidge, the president of the United States. Who would have thought?

We were winding up our tour here in New York

City, and I don't mind saying I was dog-tired. After all, I was thirteen years old, not exactly a pup. Sepp had promised us that this would be our last show. It would also be our biggest. They threw this shindig in a place called Madison Square Garden, a giant ice rink set inside what must have been the biggest building in the entire world. Peering down at us were all these bright, eager faces, more than I had ever seen in my life. We were all feeling just a mite jittery.

"It is okay, boys and girls," Sepp told us in that soothing voice of his. "They are a friendly mob."

The crowd made a deep rumbling sound, like white water boiling down the Yukon River. Some of the old excitement stirred in me as Sepp stepped onto the sled and grabbed the handlebar.

He made a clucking sound with his tongue.

I knew my signal when I heard it. I jumped into my harness and pulled the gang line taut.

Beside me, Fritz grumbled, *Aw, Chief! Do we have to?*

I nipped him one good on the shoulder. *You bet your plumed tail we do! It's what Sepp wants. And if it makes Sepp happy, I'm happy.*

Behind us, Matte and Nurmi growled, *If we have to do this, so do you, Fritz.* For good measure Nurmi bit Fritz's tail.

Fritz yelped and leapt to. After that, we trotted out onto the ice all nice and pretty. We'd show these city folks how it was done. I picked up the pace. We bounded across the ring, whipping Sepp's sled behind us. The crowd went crazy. I could tell Sepp was loving it. Truth to tell, my man Sepp was a bit of a ham when he got in front of a big crowd. And me? I was just warming up. The ice was as slick and smooth as the first freeze on Norton Sound. I led the team round and round, faster and faster— swing dogs, team dogs, wheel dogs, lead dogs—

all twenty of us scrambling to bank those sharp turns. The crowd was roaring. My heart was pounding. This was almost as fun as racing for the winners' cup.

Until I led us smack-dab—*crunch*—into a wall. We wound up all tangled in a pile of wriggling fur.

I heard a disgusted snort. It was Sugruk, one of the wheel dogs, who was lying on her side with a paw wedged in my face. *Nice work, Chief,* she said.

*Yeah, well,* I sighed. *They shouldn't ought to have put that wall there.*

Sepp laughed as he untangled us. The audience laughed, too. It wasn't a mean laugh. It was an aren't-they-the-cutest-little-doggies-you've-ever-seen kind of laugh. I'd heard it before on this trip. *Cute?* The finest racing dogs in the world? *Grrrrr.*

Once Sepp had gotten us all sorted out, he drove us back into the center of the ring. A hush fell over the crowd. A man came out on the ice. Like Sepp, he was dressed in a parka. His hood was rimmed with wolverine fur. His mukluk boots were made of sealskin.

He looked familiar. I held my nose up and got a good whiff of him. I picked up the bay leaf in his hair oil, the ink on his fingertips, the sweat on his feet, and a hint of whale blubber on his parka. It was good old Roald Amundsen from up north!

Amundsen was a big-deal explorer. He loved huskies. He thought we pretty much hung the moon. He had this scheme to go as far north as anyone had ever been, to a place folks called the North Pole. And guess how he was going to get there? You got it! With a team of huskies. And not just any huskies: Siberians. Amundsen leaned over me. I thought for a minute he was going to scratch my head and invite me to head up north with him. But instead, he draped a cold, heavy chain around my neck.

"Ladies and gentlemen," he said in a loud voice, "I would like you to meet the most extraordinary dog I have ever had the privilege of knowing.

Leonhard Seppala here calls him 'fifty pounds of muscle and fighting heart.' But I call him a hero. This gold medal is a meager reward for all that he did in the Serum Run of 1925. He played the key role in bringing much-needed medicine to the sick children of Nome."

A reward? To me, a nice reward was a pot of salmon and seal oil or whale blubber and oats bubbling over a fire. I sniffed the chain. It didn't smell like much. I couldn't eat it or chase it. It was just like those sled-racing trophies back at Sepp's place. A useless hunk of metal. The crowd cheered. I yawned and sat on my haunches. I had a feeling this fellow was fixing to talk the hind leg off a mule.

I was right. Amundsen went on and on. "It was another dog, however, that got all the credit for the run. He was hailed as a hero the world over. There is even a bronze statue of him in your very own

Central Park. You have probably heard of him. His name is Balto."

Folks murmured and nodded. Of course they knew Balto. Everybody knew Balto.

Everywhere I went, it was *Balto this* and *Balto that*. Truth to tell, I knew Balto well enough. He was in my kennel. He was owned, bred, raised, and trained by Sepp, same as I was. Sepp called Balto nothing but a scrub freight dog. Don't get me wrong, he was a nice-enough fellow. But he was no racer. And he didn't have a whole lot going on upstairs. What he had was luck. It was luck, pure and simple, that he happened to be leading the team that made the last leg of the Serum Run.

Where was I while Balto was being hailed as the bushy-tailed hero? After I did my bit in the relay, I cut loose and ran off to chase reindeer. And, let me tell you, it was a whole lot more rewarding than having a bunch of strangers shake my paw and snap my photograph for the newspapers.

Amundsen's voice rose to a shout: "Ladies and gentlemen, I give you the *real* hero of the Serum Run! I give you the one and only Togo the sled dog!"

The crowd went wild. The photographers did, too. When I had blinked away the spots from all those flashlamps, I looked over at Sepp. He was grinning, his teeth white in his sunburned face. I was glad for him. Did I care about being a hero? Did I care about medals or statues or pictures in newspapers? Nope. Not on your tintype. But Sepp cared. He cared a whole bunch. It broke his heart that another dog got all the credit for that famous run. And if Sepp's heart ached, mine did, too.

"It is true!" Sepp said when the crowd had piped down. "Balto and his team ran fifty-three miles compared to Togo's ninety-one—not counting the one hundred sixty-nine additional miles

Togo ran from Nome to Shaktoolik to pick up the serum. This is the dog who really saved those sick kids."

Poor Sepp. For the rest of my life—and probably his, too—he tried to set the record straight.

But records didn't matter to me. I'll tell you what mattered. Pulling a sled. Leading a team. Sniffing out the scent of the trail under a deep blanket of snow. That was the stuff that mattered. If you would care to hear the story of a hard-working dog who loved to run, who wasn't a hero to anyone but his musher, then you've come to the right place. But I give you fair warning: I didn't start out in life as a hero. I started out as a furry-faced little brat.

## BAD DOG TOGO

I was born in 1913 in the kennel Sepp managed for Jafet Lindeberg, his buddy from the old country. Jafet was a partner in the Pioneer Mining Company. The kennel was in Little Creek, near the city of Nome, way up north in what was then known as the Alaska Territory. My sire, or daddy, was Suggen (SOO-gin). He was a mix of Siberian husky and Alaskan malamute, and Sepp's best lead dog. My dam, or momma, was Dolly. She was the prettiest little Siberian you ever did see, one of the first to come across the Bering Strait to Alaska.

As a breed, we Siberians are a touch on the runty side. We're about half the size of malamutes. Malamutes! *Grrrrr.* Why does everybody flip for that breed? I guess because they're big. And furry—as soft and fluffy as a lady's muff. We might not be as pretty as those ladies' muffs. A man once called us "plume-tailed rats." But we're fast and have good trail sense. One way or the other, a Siberian team gets the job done. But truth be told, I almost didn't make any team myself.

When I was born, I had no littermates, no brothers and sisters. It was just little old me. With only one pup, my momma didn't have anything better to do than to worry about me. And I guess I gave her plenty to worry about.

Jafet would come to the kennel and look me over. "Dolly, how did you whelp such a small and sickly pup?"

*Hey,* I wanted to tell him. *You don't have to get personal.*

I didn't need him saying I was sickly. I knew it. To get in the pink, I knew I had to drink milk. But milk hurt my throat going down. I'd make a hocking sound and choke it back up.

"Sepp, this dog is a lost cause," Jafet said. "You take him. See what you can do with him."

I liked Sepp from the start. He had a sweet, singsong voice that was easy on the ears. And he smelled like dog fur blowing in the north wind. "You are so small. Even for a Siberian. But I am small, too. Who knows? They say that good things come in small packages."

In those first few weeks of my life, I did my best to keep my milk down. But I was forever hocking it up. My throat burned. Sepp shook his head sadly. Even then, if Sepp was sad, I was sad. Was it because I couldn't keep my milk down? After a few weeks, Sepp went away shaking his head and didn't come back.

*Why doesn't Sepp visit me anymore?* I asked my momma.

She said, *He doesn't think you've got it.*

*What's "it," Momma?*

*"It" is whatever it takes to be a sled dog, Togo. The life of a sled dog is tough. You're a tender little pup who can't keep down his momma's milk.*

*But I do* have *it!* I said. I suckled my milk. And when I hocked it up, I suckled more. I knew if I didn't keep the milk down, I'd never grow up to be a sled dog. My throat got so sore and swollen, some days I squeaked instead of barked.

Then Sepp's mate, Constance, came to the kennel. I knew she was Sepp's mate because she smelled like him, only sweeter.

"Dolly, do you mind if I take your pup with me?" she asked my momma in a gentle voice. "I promise I'll do my best to fix whatever ails him."

Constance carried me into her house, where it was warm and toasty. She sat with me on her lap in a rocking chair by the fire. She wrapped something hot around my neck. It soothed me and made my throat stop hurting. From that day on, she came and got me after I had suckled my milk.

She wrapped the hot towel around my neck and sat with me in the rocking chair. The milk began to go down and stay down without hurting. As you might expect, I got bigger.

I was five weeks old when I had my first meat. I licked it off Constance's finger. It went down easy and made my belly so happy my tail thumped against her arm.

*More! More! More!*

She wrapped my throat again. After that, I got to eat solid food every day. Now I had two mommas—the one who gave me milk, and the one who gave me meat.

No one ever figured out what was wrong with my throat. All they knew was that, by and by, it got better. Eventually, I stopped hocking and didn't need the towel anymore. I started eating salmon and ground beef with the rest of the dogs. This gave me a new problem—keeping the bigger dogs away from my bowl. I was too small to fight them off, so you might say that the very first race I ever ran was for grub! On your mark, get set, chow down!

The kennel Sepp kept us dogs in was a shack surrounded by a yard with a high wire fence. We spent most of our time out in the kennel yard, soaking up the sun and tussling. But Sepp let us youngsters who weren't working yet out of the yard sometimes. Imagine! Me no bigger than a moose's sneeze and running around on my own!

"They have got to learn about the world sooner or later," Sepp would say to the folks who thought he was plum loco.

I learned, all right. I learned to roll in Dead Things. I learned not to poke my nose into Porky Pines. I learned how to chase down a rabbit and feed myself. And most important of all, I learned about ice.

Take river ice: it could be as clear as window glass, yet still strong enough to hold my weight. Beneath the ice I'd see fish swimming around. I couldn't get at them. It used to drive me wild.

Then there was sea ice. Now that was some tricky stuff. The ice that was attached to the shore was as safe and solid as the land. But floating ice could be deadly. An onshore breeze could stir up the water and blow those cakes out to sea. And the sea was a dark, wet, cold place where sled dogs didn't go if they knew what was good for them.

Once, I wandered inland to the Great Forest. The trees there were so tall I couldn't see the tops. I met up with a big, fat, furry four-legged thing rooting around in a berry patch. She had two little ones with her, half my size. I ran up to them and crouched down with my butt in the air.

*Hey there! Let's play!* I said.

The big, fat, furry thing rose up on her hind

legs and roared. She towered over me, all bared teeth and bristling claws.

*Get away from my babies!* she snarled.

*Whatever you say, lady,* I whimpered as I backed off and skulked away. I might have been a brat, but I was no dope!

I cut and ran until I was so deep in the Great Forest, I lost the scent of the sea. I spent the night in that place, curled up with my nose in my tail. I don't think I shut my eyes once all night. How could I with all the new noises and smells, none of them very friendly? As soon as the sun rose, I hightailed it out of there and down the shoreline to home.

Sepp's kennel helper, Ole, was the first to see me. "So you decided to come back?" he said as he let me into the yard.

The other dogs came over, sniffing.

*You've been out wandering. Where have you been,*

*boy?* Suggen said. *You smell like leaf rot.*

*Leaf rot?* said Big Mary with a disapproving snort. *The kid smells like Grizzly Bear! He's lucky he's still alive!*

So that was a Grizzly Bear. *Gulp.* I flopped down in the yard. Morning chow was over, but I didn't care. I was just glad to be back home and in one piece.

My ears pricked up at the sound of Sepp's sweet, slow, singsong voice. "There you are! I was so worried about you!" He came loping into the yard and made right for me. He got down on one knee and took my head in his hands. Resting his chin on my head, he held me until I felt like nothing in the world—Grizzly Bears included—could ever hurt me.

From that day on, this would be our Man-Dog Hug. I never saw him give it to another dog. It was our thing, private-like. When he finally pulled away, his pale eyes held mine. "Did you have your-self a big adventure?"

I howled a little and told him about the Grizzly Bears and my dark night in the forest.

"You will be all right," Sepp said, ruffling my fur. "You are one tough little husky dog."

Sepp took a team out most days to do jobs, like hauling freight or carrying passengers for the min-ing company. He came into the yard early every morning. He had his own way of working, and in all the years I was with him, it never changed. The first thing he did was to lay the lines and harnesses on the ground. When the dogs saw this, they got so worked up they couldn't keep still.

"Okay, boys and girls, who wants to take a run with me today?" Sepp asked.

*Pick me! Pick me!* the dogs yowled, and leapt in the air.

Sepp went around, grabbing dogs and leading

each one over to a harness. Straddling the dog, he would slip the harness over its head and fit its two front legs through the holes. I would sit and watch while he harnessed up anywhere from eight to eighteen lucky dogs, depending on the length of his run and the size of his load.

More than anything, I wanted him to choose me. I was only a few months old, but I thought I was big enough to pull a sled. To let Sepp know how I felt, I lifted my paw when he came past me.

*I know I'm small,* my eyes said, *but I'm tough.*

"Sorry, Togo," Sepp said. "You are too small to run with the team."

He was one to talk. Sepp was small, too. Smaller than most men. But he was tough and scrappy, with eyes the color of ice. I wanted to show him I was made of the same stern stuff. While he hitched up the dogs, I'd run around and bother them. Nothing serious. I'd nip at their ears. When they'd try to nip me in return, I'd leap out of their reach and dance around on the snow. No two ways about it: I was a flat-out brat. But I was young and foolish and aching to be part of the team.

Sometimes my shenanigans would cause the dogs to get their lines all messed up. Then Sepp would have to untangle them. This vexed him no end.

"Togo, you are one pesky little rascal," he'd say. "Now git!"

No sooner would he shoo me away than I'd be back, bothering some other dog. I really had it in for these dogs. It was envy, pure and simple. How come they got to wear a harness and not me?

After four months of me bothering the dogs and Sepp bothering me about bothering the dogs, I guess he had reached the limit of his patience. A lady from town came out to the kennel and took a look around.

"I've heard such wonderful things about your Siberian huskies," she said to Sepp. "I know they can pull a sled, but do they make good house pets?"

Sepp got a real impish light in his eye. "House pets?" he said. "They would make terrific house pets, especially this dog here. His name is Togo."

Before I could lay low, Sepp reached over and grabbed me by the scruff of my neck.

"Togo, say hello to this nice lady from town."

He held me up to her face. I guess he wanted to show I wasn't going to nip her. I admit, I liked ladies. Constance had taken good care of me when I was hurting. So I gave this lady's face a lick. She tasted different from Constance. She was salty. I could tell she lived by the sea.

And that's how I began my short but sweet life as a pet.

Town Lady took me home with her. She made me a bed of blankets in the corner of her parlor.

*My own blankets?* The only blanket I'd ever known was the warm body of another dog snuggled next to me in the kennel.

"You sleep here, Togo, and keep off the couch," my new mistress told me with a big smile on her face.

She served my chow three times a day in a fancy silver dish. The chow was fancy, too. It was People Meat, like T-bone steaks and calves' livers with lots of salt. Town Lady sure knew her way around a cookstove, I'll give her that. I had never eaten so well in my life, and I didn't have to wolf it down to keep another dog from stealing it. Twice a day she took me out on a rope so I could make my mark in the snow (if you catch my drift). The rest of the time I spent on her couch.

At first, she told me to get down. "Togo, you know you're not allowed on the furniture."

But the way she said it, all soft-voiced and

smiley-faced, I knew she didn't really mean it. So I stayed on the couch, and after a while, she stopped telling me to get down. I looked out the window at the main street of Nome, which in winter was as empty as an abandoned claim. Those rare times when someone passed by, I'd put my forepaws up on the window and call out to them. When we Siberians bark, we sometimes make a *woo-woo* sound. Other times, when we're really worked up, we howl. I'd woo at the people passing, except for when they had a dog with them. When I saw a dog, I'd lift my nose. *Take me with you, brother! Take me with you, sister!* I'd howl.

The dogs could hear me, but they couldn't smell me. Where was I? They'd search everywhere with their eyes, then give up and go away. When that happened, I'd leap down from the couch and scramble to another window. *Over here!* I'd shout. *Come back!*

Once, Town Lady tried to comfort me when I kicked up too much of a ruckus. "There, there, Togo."

I looked up and woo-wooed, *Don't you understand? I can't live like this.*

"Oh, Togo. You just need a little attention." She got down on her knees and tried to rub my ears. Nobody got to touch my ears, except for maybe Sepp. I growled and snapped at her.

She pulled away and shot to her feet. "Bad dog, Togo!" she said. "Go to your bed!"

I ducked my head and skulked back to my corner. I felt lower than a weasel's belly in a gully. How could I have snapped at that nice Town Lady like that? What would Sepp have said?

One day, Town Lady was off somewhere when I heard the pitter-patter of dog feet and a whooshing sound outside. I ran to the window. A dogsled came gliding down the street, and I guess

something in me snapped. The sight of that sled filled me with such an ache, I couldn't stand it. I leapt over the back of the couch and jumped clean through the parlor window. The glass shattered like ice all around me. I stopped to shake the slivers out of my fur, and then I was off. I ran all the way back to the kennel. It was a long run, but my nose told me the way.

I arrived at the yard eager and out of breath. Ole was outside scooping up frozen poop.

*Here I am!* My plume tail was standing on end

as I peered through the wire fence, panting.

Ole came out and caught me by the scruff. He shook me hard. "What do you think you are doing, Togo? You do not belong here anymore!"

*Oh, yes, I do!*

He stared at me and scowled.

*Please don't make me go back to Town Lady!* I begged.

But he wouldn't listen. He picked me up and took me back to Town Lady's house. I felt so all-fired embarrassed I wanted to crawl up Ole's sleeve. There was my mistress in the front yard, watching a man fit new glass in the window I had smashed to bits.

She didn't say a word about the broken window. She clasped her hands to her face. There were tears in her eyes. "You found Togo!" she said to Ole. "I was so afraid I'd lost him."

Well, if that didn't beat all. Here I had busted

to bits her pretty front window and she still wanted me back! But it was going to be on her terms. From then on, I was going to stay outside the house, in her front yard, chained to a post.

"It'll be better for you out here, Togo," she said.

*Better for your windows, you mean. Better for your couch cushions.*

Looking back, I have to say that the front yard was a sight better than the parlor. And the line attached to my collar let me go to the edge of the yard. But it was a heavy chain, and it was noisy as a string of tin cups. I lasted two days like that, rattling around in the front yard. Then I snapped the chain and—can you guess?—made the long run home to the kennel.

"Togo! Back again?" Ole said. He dragged me into the kennel yard. He shut me in and went to the house. He came back with Sepp. Just the sight of that little man put a big grin on my face.

Sepp had been eating. He had grease on his mouth. He stomped over to me. The look on his face wiped the grin clean off mine. What do I always say? If Sepp was unhappy, I was unhappy.

"What am I going to do with you?" Sepp said.

My ears drooped. *Aw, Sepp, I want to be with you! You're ace high in my deck.*

Sepp scowled. I dropped to the ground. If Sepp didn't want me, I was sunk.

Suddenly, Sepp fell to his knees and grabbed me. He pressed his chin to the top of my head. My tail thumped on the ground. If Sepp was giving me our special Man-Dog Hug, my bacon was saved.

"Okay, fellow," he said in a voice that was soft and happy. "You have made your feelings clear. You can stay. In fact, I have missed you, you little rascal."

I lifted my muzzle and licked every last bit of grease off his face. How I loved that little man!

## MORE NERVE THAN BRAINS

"Okay, boys and girls, who wants to take a run with me today?" Sepp asked. Every morning when he came to the kennel to muster the team, I raised my paw. But time after time, Sepp passed up another golden opportunity.

"Not yet, Togo," he'd say. "You are still too young."

*But I'm not,* my eyes would plead. *I'm six months old! Give me just one chance, and I'll prove it to you!*

Sepp wasn't totally heartless. He did let me run

alongside the sled when he went out on shorter errands. I'd run in circles around the team. Then I'd swoop in and take a nip at someone's ear, leaping away before they could nip me back.

"You are not being very helpful, Togo!" Sepp would scold. "Why not make yourself useful and break trail for us?"

*I can do that!* I'd run ahead and wade through the drifts to find the trail. Sometimes it was hidden deep under the snow and ice, but I always found it. I'd smell the dogs who'd taken that route over the last few weeks. I'd smell their musher, and if they had carried food in their sled, I'd smell that, too: bacon and rice, coffee beans and tea leaves. If the snow wasn't too deep, the team would follow behind me. If it was very deep, Sepp would come up alongside me and tamp it down with his big, flat snowshoes.

Sometimes, however, I'm ashamed to admit

that I shirked my duty. I'd cut loose and chase a rabbit or a flock of birds, veering far off the trail.

When I did that, the lead dog would say to the team, *Togo's onto something good! Follow him!*

And the whole team would pelt after me. Even then, I guess you could say I was a leader. Sometimes Sepp didn't mind because it got the dogs running together at a nice clip. But he hated when I made them run fast over rocky ground. Once, the sled went zooming over a ledge, and it took Sepp half a day to dig it out and get the lines back into apple-pie order.

When Sepp lost his temper, we did, too, growling and snapping at each other. A bad mood was like a disease—easy to catch and hard to shake.

Sometimes I'd see another dog team on the trail, either coming our way or gaining on us from behind. That really steamed me. This was our trail! What did they think they were doing? I would head them off and go right up to the lead dog, hotheaded as all get-out.

*I've got a beef with you!* I'd snarl at the dog, who was a lot older and wiser and, more often than not, tougher than I was. But what did I know? I was a bratty little pup. *You've got no business on this trail. I can outlead you any day, and I'm not even wearing a harness!*

"Get back here, Togo, and leave those dogs be!" Sepp would holler.

When that didn't work, Sepp would pick me up and fling me over his shoulder like a sack of spuds.

*Look at the big, tough leader now!* the other dogs would laugh as Sepp carried me back to his sled.

*Just never you mind!* I'd growl at them over Sepp's shoulder. *I'll get you next time.*

Then one day, a team of eighteen malamutes came dashing across the drifts, headed straight for us. These weren't pretty, fluffy dogs. They were some mean-looking customers: tough and trail-hardened, and if their coats had once been clean, they sure weren't anymore. Their leader had one pale eye and one that was frosted over where a polar bear had taken a swipe at him. I found out later that his name was Ghost, and I should have known to steer clear of him.

I jumped in his face and bared my teeth. *Beat it!* I growled. *This is my trail!*

*Oh, you think so, do you?* said Ghost. And he leapt at me and pinned me on my back in the snow. Only Sepp was allowed to get me on my back! I was mad, but I was also scared. Ghost was twice my size. It would have been easy for him to grab hold of my throat and rip it open with his teeth. I wiggled on my back in the slippery snow, trying to slide out of his reach. But his musher kept him on a long lead, and he stuck to me like a burr. Behind him, his team was yanking at their necklines, spoiling for a fight, yodeling and yipping. If anybody tells you malamutes are quiet dogs, don't you believe them! They make plenty of noise. They grumble and snort and yip and chirp, and these were all saying the same thing: *Get him, Ghost!*

"Togo, no!" Sepp shouted at me.

The dogs on our team had a different idea.

They set up quite a ruckus. *Get him, Togo!* they howled.

Ghost held me down. Then he said to his harness mate, Stash, *Why not show this mangy upstart who's boss?*

Stash snarled and jumped at my face. I snapped at him. He snapped back. I gnashed my teeth, and he gnashed his. I went for his ears, but he got one of mine first. Stash gave a deep warning growl. *Don't move, tough guy. I've got you by the ear!*

I froze. Stash's jaws were fastened around my ear. Ghost was on my chest. Both teams of dogs fell silent. I waited for Stash's jaws to get tired. I waited for Ghost to scratch an itch. At the slightest movement from either of them, I would slip away and save myself. It was time to pull in my horns and turn tail.

That was when the two mushers stepped in.

"All right. Break it up, boys!" said Sepp.

The other musher rapped Ghost and Stash on the tops of their heads with the butt of his whip. But the dogs hung in there.

"I am sorry about this," Sepp told the musher.

The stranger said, "Your little fellow's got a lot of nerve, I'll give him that."

"More nerve than brains, I am afraid to say," Sepp muttered under his breath.

Stash and I exploded in snarls. I squirmed out from underneath Ghost and wrenched my head free of Stash's jaws.

*Ouch!* I felt the pain shoot clear through me. As it turned out, Stash had bitten off the tip of my ear! I shook my head, splattering the snow with droplets of bright red. At the first smell of blood, both teams piled on. It wasn't us against them. It was every dog for itself—a furry free-for-all, a genuine Sled Dog Rumble.

The mushers finally broke up the fracas,

picking their way through the tangled lines and flinging squirming, snarling sled dogs left and right. Sepp finally uncovered me at the bottom of the pile. He lifted me up and carried me to the sled. I screamed. I felt like I'd gone nine rounds in the ring with a rabid Grizzly Bear.

"Togo, what am I going to do with you?" Sepp said. His voice scolded, but his eyes were worried. When Sepp worried, I worried. What had I gotten myself into? He wrapped me in a fur robe and laid me in the sled, where he could keep an eye on me. It took him quite some time to set the lines straight.

The team made it to the next stop without me breaking trail. After Sepp unhooked the dogs and led them into the barn, he carried me into the one-room roadhouse and bandaged me up. If you look at photographs of me, you'll see that my right ear is all raggedy. That's where Stash got a piece of me.

That night, I slept with Sepp next to the fire. But it didn't comfort me much. I hurt all over.

But more than my aches and pains, I'll tell you what really hurt: my pride.

One good thing did result from this sorry business. In the years ahead, never again would I pick a fight with dogs on another team. If they were coming toward me, I'd swing wide and give them room to pass. If they were behind me, I'd run my team hard and leave them in the dust. This was one lesson I was glad I'd learned as a youngster.

Looking back over the years, I've seen dog teams go at each other's throats, twenty or more mutts all brawling at once. Lines got so balled up, the mushers would have to cut them with jackknives, then drag their dogs apart to keep them from killing each other. The fact is, more than one dog has died of wounds from a fight. But the memory of my run-in with Ghost and his team of marauding malamutes kept me, and my team, out of trouble from that fateful day onward.

One fine morning, a few months after that incident, Sepp took off with the team for Dime Creek. Before they left, Sepp made sure I was penned up in the yard behind the eight-foot-high wire fence meant to keep us dogs in. He told Ole to lock me up for a day or two to give them time to get away.

Sepp didn't want any more messy showdowns like the one with the malamutes. He didn't know yet that I had already learned my lesson. I sat behind the fence and watched as the team pulled out. I guess you could say my expression was *hangdog*.

Ole had his eye on me. "This time, Togo, you are staying here and out of trouble."

I yawned. Dime Creek was for saps. Who needed it? Not me! Satisfied that I was content with my lot, Ole went off to do his chores. I settled down for a nap.

That night, the temperature dropped and a blizzard blew in. Was I cold? Not really. We Siberians are built for the cold. In fact, the colder it gets, the better we like it. We have two coats. The outside coat is made up of tough, wiry hairs. It keeps out the water and the wind. The inside coat is fluffy and soft and traps the warmth of our bodies close to our skin. The next time you go out in a blizzard, you might want to try wearing two layers like I do: a fluffy, warm one on the inside, and a tough, waterproof one on the outside. You'll be as snug as a Siberian!

The snow fell so thick and fast you couldn't see the tip of your snout. But I saw something in the blizzard that nobody else saw: *opportunity.*

Constance was holed up in the house. Ole was in his cabin. The other dogs were fast asleep in the kennel. But I was standing out in the snow, with the wind at my back, staring at the top of the

fence. Eight feet wasn't really so high. First, I broke loose from my tether. Did Ole really think that flimsy rope would tie me down? Then I crouched and leapt and hit the wire just shy of the top. I fell backward into the snow. I stood up and shook myself off. I turned around and walked some ways back from the fence.

This time, I got a good running start. I ran and leapt and was sailing right over the top of the fence when I felt a searing pain. I hung, head down, swinging by one leg. I'd gotten it tangled in a loose wire. The pain was something terrible. I squealed. My cries carried above the noise of the blizzard. The cabin door banged open and Ole came charging out.

"Togo! I might have known it was you. You have gotten yourself into a fine mess now!" he shouted.

*Please don't yell at me!* I whimpered. *Get me down!*

People do amazing things with those hands and fingers of theirs. He reached up and untangled my leg from the wire. He lowered me gently onto the snow to eyeball the damage. I was bleeding like a stuck pig, but I figured I'd live.

I shot up and zipped past Ole into the night. He called my name, but this was one dog who never looked back. The scent of the team was still warm beneath the drifts, and I had to hurry if I wanted to catch up.

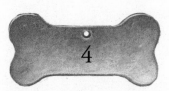

## MAKING THE TEAM

I followed the scent all day through the blowing snow. Darkness had once again fallen by the time I caught up with the team at the nearest roadhouse. There was no shelter for dogs here, so the team piled up outside the door to keep each other warm. The windows glowed with firelight.

My daddy, Suggen, was lead dog. He was on the very bottom of the heap in the warmest spot. His nose twitched, and he opened his sleepy eyes as I came near.

*Togo? I thought I caught a whiff of you. Can't say I'm surprised. You just couldn't stand being left behind, could you, little fella? Climb on and warm yourself. This blizzard is fierce.*

*No, thanks, Daddy,* I told him. *I've got plans.*

I dug a sleeping pit in the snow right next to the cabin, where the heat from the fire leaked out through a chink in the logs. I curled up with my tail over my nose. All the time I'd been running, I hadn't given a thought to my hurt leg. Now it had begun to throb. I licked it and licked it. Once it was good and clean, I settled down again and fell into a deep, exhausted sleep.

I woke up when I heard men bumping around inside. While I slept, the blizzard had covered me with a thick blanket of snow. I stood up and shook it off. I could smell chow cooking inside, but being a dog with a plan, I knew I'd best be heading out.

*See you later, brothers and sisters!* I called out

to the team. They were just digging their way out of the snow, scratching and stretching and shaking off the night's sleep.

*Take care of yourself, son!* Suggen called after me.

My plan was to get a good head start on the team. When the moment was right, I'd swoop back and show Sepp that not only had I caught up with the team, I had beat it. And to top it all, I was breaking trail for them. I'd show him how I could be just as useful on a long trip as on the shorter ones. And even more importantly, I'd show him I could stay out of trouble. Honest—I could!

The wind had settled some, but the snow was still coming down thick and fast as I picked up the trail of the last team that had traveled through these parts. I plowed, nose first, through the drifts. It was hard work, and my guts began to gurgle with hunger. Lucky for me, a rabbit crossed my path and I wolfed it down for breakfast. The sun was just trying to break through the clouds when I heard the bells on Sepp's sled handles. Thanks to me and the trail I had broken for him, Suggen was making good time. I heard Sepp talking to the dogs.

I was so happy to hear his singsong voice that I turned around and bounded back to him. I threw myself into his arms.

*It's me! I'm back! Did you miss me? Did you? Did you?*

Sepp squinted down from under his fur-lined hood: "Is that you, Togo? I was sure it was a fox ahead of us, making the team run so hard."

*Grrrr.* I was small, but way bigger than a fox. Still, I wasn't in any position to argue. Sepp set me down, and I lifted my paw in that special way of mine. *I'm ready to join the team, Sepp. What about it, old buddy, old pal?*

Sepp's face went all soft. The trusty paw routine

had done the trick. Then he noticed the gash on my leg. "Togo, what have you done to yourself?" he cried.

He swept me up and laid me down on the sled. First, he rubbed clean snow into the wound to wash it. Next, he put salve on it and wound a bandage around my leg. He set me down on the ground. I shook myself from head to tail and showed him that I felt as good as new.

That's when I got the best medicine of all. Sepp said to me, "You seem mighty determined. I guess I have no choice but to let you stay with us."

I leapt up and danced in the snow, hurt leg and all. *Thank you! Thank you! Thank you!*

After that, I settled down and got serious. I looked up into his pale eyes. *I promise you, Sepp, old man, you won't regret this.*

We ran all day through the snow and stopped that night at the next roadhouse. This one had a barn for dogs. Sepp cooked up a big pot of ground beef and oats and brought it out to us. One of the big wheel dogs tried to get at my chow.

*You're not in harness,* Ivan said. *You don't deserve this much food.*

I had caught myself a rabbit earlier in the day and I wasn't as hungry as the others, but I snapped at him all the same. I couldn't have these dogs thinking they could walk all over me.

After dinner, we lay around and talked. Nikki said, *You sure led us on a wild chase. We ran half the*

*day. I sure do hope Sepp goes easy on us tomorrow.*

*What do you mean?* Suggen said. *Sepp is the easiest musher in the territory. Have you seen the way some mushers treat their teams? They lay the whip on their dogs and starve them when they don't run fast enough. But Sepp never uses the whip unless he has to, and he always feeds us well.*

The next morning, we made an early start. The snow had stopped, the sky was clear, and the sun sparkled on the drifts. My leg felt fine so I bounded alongside the team, running ahead every so often to break trail. It was around midday when I caught a whiff of reindeer. A big whiff. It smelled like a whole herd. Well, a dog's got to do what a dog's got to do. I took off after the scent. The team took off, too. The brakes on Sepp's sled couldn't hold them back.

My preferred way of moving was in a straight line. I didn't care if it took me through deep snow, over icy rivers, or down rocky hillsides. All I knew was that straight was the fastest way to get from here to there. And if straight was where the reindeer were, that was where I was going! I leapt over a stand of willows and headed off the trail. The team followed and got socked in by a deep snowbank.

I left them behind. Those reindeer led me on a crazy chase. Somewhere along the frozen river, I lost the scent. I went all over, trying to find it, but finally gave up and headed back. You can't win them all.

Sepp had just finished digging the team out of the drift when I showed up. I knew he was going to be vexed with me for running the team into the bank. I ducked my head and skulked up to him.

*I'm a bad dog,* I wooed.

He frowned and looked down at me with his hands on his hips. "There is only one thing to do with a dog like you," the old man growled.

*Uh-oh,* I thought. *I'm in for it now.*

"Let us hitch you up to the sled and harness some of that energy."

I was one happy little mutt. At last! The moment I had been waiting for all my life!

Sepp buckled me in next to Ivan, right in front of the sled. This is what is known as the wheel position. The wheel dogs provide the power. I'd show Sepp that I had muscles made of iron, even though I was only eight months old and had a bandage on my leg.

Sepp stepped onto the back of the sled. He made a clucking noise with his tongue. It was our signal to go.

Up ahead, Suggen leaned into his harness and pulled the gang line taut. The rest of us followed. And off we went. We ran mile after mile of snowy track, following Suggen's lead. My paw pads warmed up and my claws dug into the snow.

My legs churned. For the first time in my life, I was filled with a sense of purpose. I was a part of the team now. There were eight of us dogs running like one big dog with many legs, whipping the sled along behind us. I was born to do this.

I heard the shushing sound of Sepp putting on the brakes. "Whoa!" he called to us.

We stopped. The gang line went slack. The silence of the snowy landscape settled around us. We panted, fogging the air with our breath. Sepp stepped off the sled and came to me.

"Good work, Togo!" he said. "You are not even winded. Now let us see what you can do farther up the line."

He unhooked me from the wheel position and moved me up the line with the swing dogs. These dogs listen for cues from either the musher or the lead dog. Then they shift in their tracks to move the team through turns. If the swing dogs don't do

their job smoothly, everything falls apart. A team can lose its balance. The dogs can pile up on top of each other, the lines can get tangled, and the sled can spill over. I pricked up my ears and waited for Sepp's commands.

"Haw!" Sepp called out.

You might wonder how I knew right off what he meant. It was from all the times I had run alongside the sled. Then again, maybe I was just born knowing. But I knew that *haw* meant to turn left. I moved my right shoulder over and crossed my right paw over my left. Along with my teammate,

we shifted the sled toward the left, following the bend in the trail past a stand of willows.

A little while later, Sepp called out, "Gee!"

I knew this meant to turn right. Since I was on the right side of the team, this was easier for me to do than turning left. I simply pointed my nose right, shifting my weight to the right side. We made the turn smoothly, running past a row of big boulders. I liked this job even better than being a wheel dog. But the job I had my eye on was farther up the line.

Then it was like Sepp had read my mind. He

took me out of the swing section and moved me up to the very front of the line, in Suggen's place, right next to a dog named Russky.

*This is a proud day for me, son,* Suggen said.

"Maybe I am crazy," Sepp said as he hooked me up at the head of the team. "But I think you are ready."

*You don't mind, do you?* I asked Russky.

*Watch and learn, kid,* Russky said. *Watch and learn.*

Learning wasn't hard. I saw Russky doing what I did when I was running free. Sniffing out the trail and staying on it. I had a good nose on my face. Sometimes I found the scent of the trail when he was heading off in the wrong direction.

*You're a natural,* said Suggen, who ran alongside the sled.

It wasn't long before Sepp let me take over the lead. That was when Sepp discovered my fondness for straight lines. If I knew where we were headed, and a straight line was the shorter route, I'd run the straight line. But that could get us bogged down in snow. It was one thing for me to dig myself out. It was another for a whole team to do it.

Digging out was hard work for Sepp, and it took time. When Sepp lost time, he got sad. When Sepp was sad, I was sad. When I saved Sepp time by not getting us stuck in the first place, he was happy. It didn't take me long to learn to stick to the trail.

At the end of the day, Sepp gave me extra chow and a long, loving Man-Dog Hug. He said to the owner of the roadhouse, "Togo is only eight months old but he ran seventy-five miles today. I have never seen anything like it in a dog so young. I think I have found the natural leader I have been looking for."

## ICE SENSE

I was about a year and a half old and running lead, traveling from Nome to a place called Unala-kleet (YOU-nuh-luh-kleet), located across Norton Sound on the Bering Sea. When the sound froze over, going across on the ice was the best short-cut. When it was only part frozen, the next-best thing was to travel on the ice that formed along the shoreline. My job that day was to keep us on that ice. If I got us on a loose piece, the wind could blow us out to sea and we might never come back.

Sepp stood on the runners, took off a mitten, and held up his bare hand. "There is a strong breeze blowing onshore from the sea," he said. "We should be safe. What do you say, Togo?"

I put my nose down and sniffed the ice thoughtfully. Sepp knew I had pretty good ice sense. Having ice sense meant I could smell the water beneath the ice. If the smell was too strong, I knew that the ice was thin and probably not strong enough to hold us. I also kept an ear pricked for how the ice sounded. Quiet ice was solid and steady. But if it groaned or hissed, that meant it was breaking apart and dangerous. It was talking to me. It was saying, *Watch out, little dog! Stay away!* I could also feel the ice beneath my paw pads. I knew that if it was damp, it was probably not frozen through.

This ice looked and smelled and sounded and felt safe enough. I lifted my eyes to Sepp's. *I got no problem with it, old man,* I told him.

Sepp nodded and clucked, and I led us out onto the frigid surface of the Bering Sea. The sun was hanging low in the sky, and it was dark and gloomy out there in the frozen wastes. I ran with my nose to the ice so I could smell suspicious changes in its thickness. My ears were cocked for sounds. I kept an eye out for cracks. Small cracks were nothing to worry about—I was looking for cracks that widened and moved toward you as if an invisible saw blade was slicing the ice.

Suddenly, I saw something dark smack-dab ahead of us. The team was going all out. The ice was slippery. I gave a loud yip, but Sepp must not have heard because he kept driving us forward. There was nothing for me to do but leap up into the air and throw myself onto the dogs behind me, blocking their forward movement with the weight of my body.

*What the heck?* they grumbled as they scrambled to a halt and nipped at me. *Get off us, Chief!*

"What is all this nonsense, boys and girls?" Sepp called out. He climbed off the sled and came to stand over me. "Togo, what is the meaning of this?"

I scrambled out of the heap and pointed my nose toward the black thing ahead of us.

Sepp peered through the gloom. Then he slapped his forehead.

Directly ahead of us was a dark channel of sea-water. I had stopped just short of running into it. Sled dogs and sleds sink fast in seawater.

I knew what had happened. The wind had changed direction and was now blowing the ice away from the shore. Instead of being on solid ice, we were now on a loose island. And the wind was blowing our ice island out to sea. We were in one big heap of trouble.

I stared at the widening channel. The ice on the other side looked solid and safe. How to get over there was the question.

*Come on, Chief. Get us out of this fix!* the dogs whined. They sank onto their haunches and started panting. I looked to Sepp. He was frowning deeply. He was as worried as the rest of us.

"What do you think, Togo?" he said.

I whimpered, *I think we're sunk, buddy.*

Sepp wiped the ice out of his eyes and looked

around. Suddenly, he brightened. "I just might have it!" he said.

I stood by as he put a long lead line on me, making sure that I was still hooked up to the team. Then he picked me up. I thought he was going to hug some heat into my bones. Instead, like I was a piece of cargo, he heaved me across the channel! I landed on my tail on the other side and scrambled to my feet.

*Are you kidding me?* I howled in outrage. What had gotten into him? Had he lost his marbles? Had I done something to get his goat? On the other side of the channel, the dogs had lined up, noses pointed toward me.

*What are you doing over there? What's the old man up to now?* they howled.

I didn't like this any more than they did. I ran up and down the edge of the ice, looking for a way to get across.

"Stay where you are, Togo!" Sepp called to me. "Turn around—and run!" He pointed with both arms toward the shore.

So that was the plan! Why didn't he say so in the first place? I turned around and tugged the lead line taut. Then I began to pull with all my might. My claws dug into the ice, and I took one trembling step at a time. If I hauled hard enough, I would pull the ice island—with the sled and the team on it—across the channel to the safer ice where I stood.

After a while, the team caught on. They were all charged up, yipping encouragement. *Keep going!* they called. *You can do it! We know you can!*

Sepp's sweet, singsong voice urged me on. "Great work, Togo! You are closing the gap. Good dog! Keep pulling! Whatever you do, do not stop!"

I had the gap nearly closed when the unthinkable happened!

The lead line snapped, and I fell nose first into the ice. The team tumbled backward and started squalling and whimpering as the ice island floated away. I ran back and forth, howling fit to bust.

*Help, Sepp!* I called out. *What now?*

Sepp stared across at me, his shoulders slumped. I could tell the old man was fresh out of ideas.

In that moment, I knew I had no choice. I belonged with Sepp and the team. Even if they were headed out to sea on a floating island of ice, my place was with them. I jumped into the icy water.

*Freezing! Freezing! Freezing!*

At first, it was so cold I was too stunned to swim. Then I came to my senses and my legs started churning. Somehow, they carried me across the channel to the island.

Sepp reached down and caught the loose line around my neck. He hauled me up onto the ice. I was so excited to be back with my team that I jumped for joy, rolling around in the snow. Soon, my sopping fur was completely coated in ice and snow and slush. I struggled to sit up. I was all weighted down with ice. I couldn't even lift a paw. *Help!* I whimpered. *I'm stuck in a parka of ice!*

Sepp laughed until he almost cried. "Togo! Look at you—what a mess!" He took off his mittens and began picking big clumps of ice off me. But it wasn't long before his fingers began to turn blue. He had to stuff his hands back into his mittens. Meanwhile, the ice island was floating out into the cold, dark sea. I stood up and shook myself from nose to tail. More big pieces of ice came flying off me.

I ran to my place at the head of the line. *Sepp, old man, put me back in harness. We can't just stand here and float out to sea. We've got to keep moving.*

Sepp hooked me up again, but he couldn't help laughing. "You look like a polar bear cub," he said.

*Never you mind what I look like, old man! It's what I can do that counts.* I started leading the team along the edge of the ice island, making sure I kept the shore in my sights at all times.

I kept us moving all night. Toward morning, the wind shifted. Our ice island was being blown back toward the shore.

"Eureka!" as we say in the territory. At last, I saw what I had been looking for all night. A place where the floating ice butted up against the land ice. I led us, splashing, across the slushy bridge. When we got to the other side, the surface of the ice felt as solid as rock beneath my half-frozen paw pads. I let out a long, shuddering sigh of relief.

"Good dog, Togo! I knew you could do it!" Sepp called as I led the team rip-tearing across the ice toward the shore.

When we got to the roadhouse that night, Sepp tossed an extra ration of seal oil into the dog salmon he cooked us. He gave me the first taste. I gobbled it up and looked to Sepp for more. He gave it to me.

"You deserve seconds tonight, Togo. You are a remarkable dog. I owe you my life. We all do."

I shook off the compliment and swallowed my seconds. I was full as a tick and one happy Siberian. I had outsmarted the sea ice. I had a belly full of seal oil. And the pads of my paws were even beginning to thaw.

## OFF TO THE RACES

I wasn't much older than two years when Sepp really began to get the racing bug. Whenever we weren't working, he started taking us out on empty runs. That meant we didn't have any freight to carry or any destination in mind. He was just looking to see how fast we could go. Sepp knew we could pull heavy loads. He knew we could go long distances without resting or eating. But speed had never been all that important to Sepp. Now, suddenly, speed was everything. We could feel his excitement each time we went out. We caught it. We ran over unbroken and unknown trails. We ran off into the wilderness, where only moose and reindeer witnessed our performance.

When Sepp clucked, I turned to the dogs behind me and yipped, *The old man wants speed. Let's show him what we can do.* When the dogs followed my lead, I was happy and so was Sepp. When the dogs dragged their feet, I'd circle around on my lead line and nip at them.

*Speed it up, slowpokes!* I'd tell them. That usually did the trick.

Sepp drove us out every day, and every day he took us a little farther away. We learned to go fast all day long. And because the faster we went the happier Sepp got, we pushed ourselves. Our paws got hard and our muscles even harder.

After a few months of this, he changed our route and started running us on the same trail every time. He called it the Sweepstakes Trail. It was two days out and two days back.

"I want you boys and girls to learn this trail inside out and upside down."

One morning, after Sepp hitched us up, he and Ole loaded the sled with big cans. The cans were sealed, but I knew what was inside of them: moose meat. As we made our way along the Sweepstakes Trail, we stopped every so often so that Sepp could remove one of the cans from the sled and bury it in a snowdrift. I fretted. It seemed like a terrible waste of chow.

But Sepp said, "Do not worry, Togo. We will be back here during the race. I will dig up that meat and feed you what is inside. That way you will not have heavy cans bogging you down in the race."

Several nights later, after he had thrown down our food in the kennel yard, Sepp clapped his hands loudly. We looked up from our chow. "Are you boys and girls ready to race tomorrow?"

A few of us lifted our heads and yipped, then returned to our bowls.

"What is this?" Sepp said. "Where is your team spirit? Are we going to win this race, or are we going to skulk away with our tails between our legs?"

*I'm ready to race, old man, but what is this* winning *business?* I asked.

Sepp came over to me and patted his chest. That was the sign that it was okay for me to jump up on him. I reared up and propped my paws on his thighs. He lifted me and spun me around, laughing and singing and chattering in his singsong voice, "Winning is coming home with the cup. Winning is showing all those other mushers that you are the best dogs in the territory. Winning is making me the happiest musher in the world!"

The other dogs were dancing around us in a circle, begging to be picked up, too. But Sepp had

room in his arms for only one dog, and that dog
was yours truly, Togo.

*You heard him, brothers and sisters!* I called out
to the dogs. *Winning the race will make Sepp happy,*

*so that's what we're going to do.* I let out a lusty howl, and the dogs howled along with me. We would prove to those other dogs that we were winners.

Sepp showed up early the next morning. He clapped his mittens together and said, "Race day, team! Are you ready to win, Togo?"

I stood tall and wagged my tail. *I'm ready, ready, ready!*

Sepp hooked us up to a brand-new sled. It was lighter than the freight sled, with birch runners instead of hickory. We traveled light, with nothing but Sepp's rolled-up sleeping bag and a first-aid kit for man and dog. He drove us slowly into town. Nome was usually fast asleep at that hour, but that morning it was wide awake and jumping. A brass band played loud music. Bright lights were strung along Front Street. Everybody looked happy to see us. Eight other sleds were lined up in front of a red line drawn in the snow. The dogs were wild with excitement, leaping and yanking at their harnesses, raring to go. The race route was one big loop, so Nome was both our starting point and our finish line.

Sepp walked along the gang line, looking over our rig. In the last few days, he had replaced all the weak harnesses and lines and buckles. A Nome Kennel Club judge came by with a camera and flashlamp and snapped a photo of each of us dogs.

I blinked to clear my vision. *Grrrrr. Why did he do that?* I asked Suggen.

*It's all part of the racing game,* said Suggen. *Believe it or not, some mushers try to replace tired dogs with fresh ones along the course. That's against the rules. This way, they can't cheat. They have to finish the race with the same team they started off with.*

*What a crazy business! Sepp would never cheat,* I said.

*Not every musher is as honest as Leonhard Seppala,* said Suggen.

Sepp was as excited as everyone else. He said to us in a whisper, "Okay, boys and girls, we are going to start out like we have all the time in the world. We are going to take it nice and easy."

*Nice and easy?* These other dogs were ready to race. What about us? We weren't here for a stroll in the park. But Sepp had a plan, and his plan was my plan.

Sepp was just kneeling to give me the old Man-Dog Hug when a tenth sled came gliding down Front Street, drawn by a team of handsome huskies. They were all brushed out and done up in shiny harnesses. The rider on the back of the sled was dressed from head to toe in fur. As the sled drew nearer, I saw that it was a lady.

"All hail the Queen of the Sweepstakes!" one of the mushers shouted.

The crowd cheered.

Behind me, Sasha said, *I don't get it. Are those fancy dogs running, too?*

*Nah,* said Suggen. *They're just for show. She's here to signal the start of the race.*

The Queen of the Sweepstakes raised a furry mitten and waved at the crowd. I caught her scent. I knew that lady! She was my old friend Constance! Sepp's very own mate was the Queen of the Sweepstakes.

"Hello, Togo!" She waved. I pricked my ears and wagged my tail. She had a piece of cloth in her hand. She held the cloth up high and dropped it. When it hit the ground, the other dog teams leapt over the starting line. The sleds slid forward; the runners hissed over the snow. The race was on! But Sepp held us back.

"Remember, boys and girls, easy does it," he reminded us. "Save your energy for later in the race."

Sepp sat down on the sled and leaned back. When he did that, we knew he wanted to go nice and slow. I led the team forward. Ahead of us, the other drivers drove their dogs hard and fast. For them, it was *go, go, go.* For us, it was *slow, slow, slow. Grrrrr.*

It got colder. It took all of my willpower not to break into a run. But Sepp wanted us to hang back, and Sepp was the boss. Much as I hated to, I kept the poky pace all the way to the roadhouse at Cape Nome. There, we met up with some of the other teams. They had stopped to rest because they were tuckered out from running the first leg. We hadn't gone anywhere near hard enough to need rest. Sepp grabbed himself some soup, and we were off again with plenty of energy to spare. Sepp waved at some of the other mushers as we glided slowly past them.

The temperature had plunged and the snow fell. To show everyone that he was still in no rush,

Sepp got off the sled and ran alongside us, like a two-legged dog. I was glad when he got back in the sled, where he belonged. But we were still lagging behind a few of the other teams. It was plum embarrassing. I could just hear the other dogs snickering at the little slowpokes from Little Creek.

By the time we made it to the trailside cabin at Timber, the snow was up to our shoulders. The tracks of the team ahead of us were barely visible, but I could still smell them. We were aching to catch up and overtake them, but Sepp wouldn't have it. We'd barely broken into a trot all day. He wanted us to rest. We weren't even tired! *Grrrr.*

By the time we reached Council, we were truly tuckered out. Sepp dug a can of meat out of the snow and fed us. Then he put salve on our cracked paws. No one had bloody pads or broken claws. But our bellies and groins were cold and caked with snow. With little fur to cover them, our groins

were exposed to the cruel elements. Sepp brushed away the ice and wrapped rabbit fur around our middles. We had a cozy night's sleep.

The next day, just beyond the Telephone Creek checkpoint, we passed another team. They were hung up on the side of a slippery glacier.

*What happened to you?* I asked one of the dogs.

*Reindeer!* she said. *Wouldn't you just know it? We took off after them and wound up getting all tangled up for our trouble.*

After Sepp helped sort out the lines, we left them and went on ahead. I lifted my nose to the wind. There was the sweet smell of reindeer! A nice big herd. Probably the same ones that had lured those dogs onto the glacier.

*Let's go!* I said to the team, and I took off at a run. We led Sepp and his sled on a merry chase that morning, up hills and flying off ledges, the sled banging behind us. We didn't care. Sepp didn't, either, so long as we went fast and stayed on the trail and didn't bog down. But it didn't last. Finally, we got twisted up in a thicket of willows, and Sepp had to get out and help us. It took him a mighty long time to work us free. By the time we were lined up again, the reindeer scent had faded, which was too bad. But the good news was that we had plenty of energy left—and now there was only one team ahead of us.

## KING OF THE SWEEPSTAKES

We pulled in at the halfway checkpoint at Candle. We didn't need to rest, but the Kennel Club judges came out and waved at Sepp to stop. They checked us to make sure Sepp wasn't running us ragged. The judges didn't like it when mushers drove their dogs too hard. In their eagerness to win the cup, some mushers had been known to drive their dogs half to death. But the judges didn't have anything to worry about with Sepp. He treated us, as always, with great kindness. When they finished poking and peering, a judge said to him, "These dogs of yours are in amazingly good shape."

And then, suddenly, Big Mary cut loose and made a run for it. Maybe she scented a rabbit. Maybe she was just feeling frisky. But Sepp needed to catch her and bring her back or we couldn't get on with the race.

I yelled at Big Mary, *Get back here right now, you silly Siberian, or you'll ruin everything!*

A crowd of people formed a circle to trap Big Mary, but she kept slipping through their legs. I think she was enjoying the attention. Finally, Sepp ran and leapt on top of her. He caught her, all right, but Big Mary turned around and bit Sepp on the hand.

Uh-oh. The fun was over.

Sepp cried out in pain. But he didn't release his grip on Big Mary. One of the judges took over and hooked her up to the line. A doctor patched up

Sepp's hand. It turned out Big Mary had bit right through the skin to the bone. For the rest of the race, Sepp had to drive with only one hand.

On the return run to Camp Haven, we caught up with the one team that had so far outpaced us. The musher was a man named Scotty. He was the top dogsled driver in Alaska. Scotty and his team had won so many Sweepstakes races that he took it for granted he was going to win this one, too. So did his uppity dogs.

*You mutts don't stand a chance against us,* Scotty's lead dog, Baldy, said to me.

*Maybe we do and maybe we don't,* I said, yawning widely to show I didn't give a hoot one way or the other.

While Sepp dug into some moose stew, we flopped down on the snow. The spring sun was high and hot. We soaked it up through our coats and let it sink into our aching bones. A fiendish idea crept into my furry head. Maybe we'd stay here like this all day. Maybe we'd show Sepp just how good we were at taking it easy.

The next thing I knew, Scotty had come out of the cabin and was rousing his dogs. They whined and complained. *Aw, Scotty! Can't we get just a little more shut-eye?*

"There's no time to waste," Scotty said.

Sepp came bounding out of the cabin. He set about hitching us up to the sled. What had happened to taking it slow? Just to get his goat, we all grumbled.

*Aw, Sepp, we just got here!* Suggen complained.

*The sun's so warm!* Nikki yowled.

I said, *Do we have to take off so soon? It's so sweet dozing here in the warm sun. And Scotty's team probably won't get very far. Anyone with eyes can see they're plum tuckered out.*

Sepp laid out the harnesses and lines. "Up and

at 'em, boys and girls. We cannot let Scotty's team get a lead on us now," he said.

I reckon we had made our point. So I growled to the team, *Get back in harness, brothers and sisters.*

The team got in line, and Sepp hooked us up. We started out slow enough. Even slower than we had to, if you ask me. My team was holding out on me. I could feel the weight of them behind me, dragging their tails.

*What's the matter with you?* I snarled at them as I tugged on the gang line. *Now's our chance to make tracks. Do you want Scotty's dogs to beat us?*

That got them moving, and after that, we made good time, with very little urging from Sepp. The sun was bright on the snow, and in spite of his bad hand, Sepp whistled and sang along the way. The Boston checkpoint loomed into view. Scotty's team was outside the cabin, lying on their sides in the snow. They were so still, I thought they might have been dead. Sepp stopped whistling and singing. We slowed down.

"Okay, boys and girls," he told us in a heavy voice. "Here is where we act like we are beat."

We slowed down to a creep. We hung our heads as we pulled past Boston camp. Scotty came out of the cabin.

"As you can see, my dogs have had it!" Sepp called out to Scotty. "We are going to hobble along to Council and pack it in for the night."

We dragged our feet until we were out of sight. Then we picked up our pace and double-timed it all the way to the cabin at Council. We'd left Scotty thinking that Sepp had run us practically into the ground. But really we were busting to go.

At midday, I got a powerful whiff of rabbit. I took off, and the others kept up. Luckily, the rabbit was following the race trail. We ran all afternoon trying to catch that rabbit. We never caught it, but sometimes a good run is almost as satisfying as a catch.

At the Timber checkpoint, we found Scotty and his team resting. We hadn't seen them pass us so I gathered they'd taken a shortcut. There was a big barn for the dogs. Scotty's team was on one side and our team was on the other. They looked too bushed to pick a fight, but still, we kept our distance. They were a raggedy bunch and didn't look like winners to me.

Scotty kept coming out to check on his dogs, and I could tell he was worried. We were just settling in when he returned and hitched them up. They pulled away from the barn as if they were hauling a sled full of rocks. A few hours later, while we were still resting up, they came dragging back.

"We lost the trail!" Scotty said to Sepp.

Well, surprise, surprise. I'll tell you why Scotty's

team lost the trail. Because they were too tuckered out to use their noses.

Our team was as fresh as a bouquet of daisies. I stood up and wagged my tail. *Put me on it, Sepp, and I'll find that trail.*

"Rest awhile longer, Togo," Sepp said.

Grumbling, I settled back down and fell asleep.

When Sepp came out to hook us up, Scotty's team was still laid out on their sides, ribs heaving. But our team was full of vim and vigor. I led them out into the snow. Nose close to the ground, I caught the scent of the trail, and we were off. Sometime later, I heard Scotty's team behind us. They were following the trail I'd broken. But I wasn't about to let those mutts steal the lead now. I saw to it that we dashed all the way up the steep slopes of Topkok Hill.

When we got to the top, we turned and looked

back. There was no sign of Scotty and his team. Maybe they'd stopped to take another rest. Maybe we'd gotten so far ahead that they had lost the trail again. As I was thinking these thoughts, a thick blanket of fog blew in and covered the top of the mountain. Suddenly, it was hard to see the swing dogs behind me, much less Sepp and the sled.

I edged down the other side of the mountain. This was, I later learned, the dangerous blowhole of the Topkok Flats. It was steep and slick with ice, and the fog had me spooked. Rocks reared up out of the mist like giant Grizzly Bears. Sepp wasn't whistling or singing now. The dogs crept along behind me on their haunches. I heard the *drip-drip-drip* of ice melting off the rocks. It was all I could do not to imagine that the dripping sound was the watering mouths of those giant Grizzlies. From the sound of it, they were just hankering after a taste of sled dog. I decided to pick up my pace. The faster I got us through this fog, the better. Our coats were sopping wet with it. I couldn't see the dogs behind me, but I heard their nervous panting. I heard the *pat-pat-pat* of their feet and the *whoosh* of the sled runners. Then, just as I was thinking that the fog had settled in to stay, it began to thin.

*Hallelujah!*

We burst out into dazzling sunshine and clear skies.

I was so happy to be out of that fog that I ran at my fastest speed through the finest weather and terrain that Alaska had to offer. We breezed past the last three checkpoints. By then, we were so far in the lead that no one—not even Scotty and his team—could catch up to us.

I knew we were approaching the finish line in Nome when I heard the cannons booming. There were whistles blowing and the sound of folks kicking up a joyful ruckus. They greeted us with happy

faces and waving banners. Sepp raised his bandaged hand and waved back. He was smiling so hard I thought he'd crack his face. As we rode down Front Street, folks grabbed Sepp from the back of the sled and hoisted him on their shoulders. They bore him toward the judges' stand. Another man hopped on the back of our sled and drove us the rest of the way.

The judge handed Sepp the cup. He kissed it
and hugged it to his chest. Constance hugged Sepp.
The Queen of the Sweepstakes now had her king.
He held the cup high over his head and said to
the crowd, "This belongs to my incredible team—
especially my lead dog, Togo."

*Aw, shucks. 'Tweren't nothin'.* It was enough to
make a sled dog blush.

Sepp went on, "Not once during the entire run did I use my whip. I ended up with the same dogs I set out with. And all of them are in tip-top shape."

Well, I wouldn't have said tip-top, but we had no bleeding paw pads or torn claws.

I ran many a race after that and won most of them. Sepp liked to brag that I had won more races and covered more miles than any other dog in Alaska.

All in all, not bad for a little plume-tailed rat from Little Creek.

## DEATH RIDES HARD ON OUR TRAIL

We settled into a pleasant routine, me and the dogs and Sepp. Winters we worked, hauling passengers and freight from town to town. Springs we raced in the All Alaska Sweepstakes or one of the many other races that took place in the territory.

Summer was something else. You might wonder what a sled dog does when there's no snow for his sled. In my time, most dogs sat around all summer getting fat and lazy. But Sepp wouldn't have that. So he hooked us up to a wheeled cart and drove us up and down the Kougarok Valley, through the tundra.

The summer I was three years old, we worked with the miners up in the Grand Central River Valley. I tell you, that was some of the bleakest, sorriest, most dog-forsaken wilderness in all of Alaska. And that's saying something. The men dug mines and ditches. Sepp had us hauling supplies to the construction camps. Instead of pulling a sled, we pulled a pupmobile, or dogcart. Sepp hooked us up to a loaded car, and we'd haul it along the tracks to the next camp. The gravel on the line was hard on our paw pads, but we did the job.

Sometimes a moose would get on the tracks and just stand there, munching willow leaves. We would howl at it—*Move!*—but moose never paid us much mind. Sepp would wave his arms and shout and sometimes the moose would move. Sometimes, though, they'd get ornery and try to charge us. When this happened, Sepp would take out his rifle and shoot the moose. Sepp ate a lot of moose meat that summer.

The winter of my fourth year, we were hauling freight up the Koyuk River to Dime Creek. We had just arrived when a man came running toward us. He smelled of blood. It was a scent that stirred us dogs up like no other. Sepp used to say that it woke up the wolf in us. I never knew whether to run from it in fear or hunker down and lap it up. We howled as the man came closer. He was shouting and waving his arms.

"It's Bobby Brown!" the bloody man said. "You've got to help him."

I knew that name. We'd raced against Bobby Brown—and beat him—only last spring. And I knew this man, too, beneath the blood. It was Louis Stevenson, an old hand on the trail.

Stevenson went on, "Bobby's working at the

sawmill down the road and he's had a terrible accident. You have to take him to the hospital in Candle!"

Then I understood. The blood on the man didn't belong to Stevenson. It belonged to Bobby. He must have been hurt something awful to lose that much blood.

I could tell by the set of Sepp's shoulders that he was bone weary from our haul. "It must be a sixty-mile trip to Candle," he said. "My dogs have just traveled forty. Is there a driver with a fresher team nearby?"

"No!" said Stevenson. "Besides, Bobby wants you to do it. He says you're the best driver in Alaska and, even tired, your dog team is still the fastest. Only you and your dogs can do this."

Sepp turned to the team. All sixteen of us looked back at Sepp. We watched as the tiredness seemed to drain out of him. He lifted his head and pulled back his shoulders. The sparkle returned to his eyes, and he spoke to us in his most lively voice. "You heard him, team! Bobby needs us! Time to get back on the line!"

Instantly, we jumped to our feet, shaking off our weariness like so much extra fur. A sled dog likes nothing better than to be needed for a job. All any dog wants is a job to do. And the more important the job, the better. Sepp and Louis Stevenson stepped onto the back of the sled, and we hauled tail for the mill.

As soon as we arrived, Sepp hopped off and unhitched us. He hadn't eaten since Isaac's Point. He went to get himself some chow while Stevenson and the other lumbermen shoved the sled through the wide sawmill door. We sat and waited. After a time, the men pushed the sled back out. Bobby Brown was lying flat on his back in the sled, wrapped in a wolf-skin robe. His legs were splinted, and one of them looked pretty chewed up. Gently, the men tucked blankets around him.

"Thanks, boys," said Bobby.

I was surprised to hear a man so badly hurt speaking. He was even smiling.

Sepp clicked his tongue, and all sixteen of us jumped into our harnesses as one. We felt as fresh as we had that morning.

Folks must have heard about Bobby's accident, because all along the way to Candle, people came out onto the trail to watch us carry him to the hospital. Eskimos and gold miners alike greeted us in worried silence. They could tell how badly hurt Bobby was. Who among them didn't know what a tough and dangerous place the Alaska Territory was? An accident like this could have happened to any one of them. Some called out and wished us luck and fast sledding. More than a few had tears in their eyes.

Bobby smiled and waved as we passed. He thanked them for coming out to see him.

"I'll be back!" he promised. "Once they've sewn me together again."

We heard Bobby's cheerful voice ring out all

along the way, "Describe to me the landmarks, and I'll tell you if you're on the right track!"

"We are passing a stand of pines," Sepp said.

"Turn right after the pines, and follow the bend in the river," Bobby told him.

"Gee!" Sepp said. And we turned right and followed the river.

Sometimes, though, Bobby fell into long silences. When we ran over a bumpy stretch of trail, he would moan and call out, "Go easy, boys!"

Going easy across rough terrain was pretty near impossible. Much of the trail was unbroken. We swam through snow up to our shoulders. Nose first, I blazed the trail. Then Sepp had to put on his snowshoes and tamp down the snow so the sled could pass. It was a real slog.

"I just hope none of you catches the scent of a reindeer," Sepp worried aloud.

He was right about that. If we smelled reindeer,

Bobby's ride was going to get a whole lot bumpier. Lucky for him, nothing worth chasing crossed our path.

Darkness fell. It grew colder, and the snowflakes flew thick and fast. Sepp stopped us every so often to check Bobby's bandages.

"I'll be all right," Bobby said. "Just keep going."

Heads bowed before the wind, we did just that. Then, suddenly, the trail began to look familiar to me. I knew exactly where we were. Sepp noticed it, too. He jumped off the back of the sled and ran alongside me.

"Know where we are, Togo?" he asked.

I yipped. I sure did. We were on one of my favorite legs of the Sweepstakes run. I waited until the old man got back in the sled, and then I picked up speed. Not even the blizzard could slow me down now.

When the lights of Candle sparkled through the trees, I heard Sepp give out a whoop. "Hang on, Bobby!" he said. "We are nearly there."

We sped right up to the roadhouse. Sepp put on the brakes, bringing us to a skidding halt. Sepp jumped off the sled and ran into the roadhouse.

"I need help dragging a sled up to the hospital!" he shouted to the men inside.

Ten men came tumbling out the door, pulling on their parkas and mukluks. Sepp unhitched us, and the men all heaved together and pushed the sled up the hill to the hospital.

A few days later, Sepp came out to the kennel to tell us the sorry news. Bobby Brown had died in the hospital.

"Bobby Brown will never run another race," Sepp said.

Sepp was sad, so I was sad. But I also felt a little bit happy, knowing we had gotten that brave man as far as the hospital. His wife and children had gotten a chance to see him and to say their final farewells before he died.

Later, a famous poet named Mrs. Esther Birdsall Darling wrote a poem about the rescue of Bobby Brown. Sepp was so proud he stood in the kennel yard and read it aloud to us in his sweet, singsong voice. I didn't understand much of it, but I did hear my name toward the end of it.

*There's the sting and the rage of the blizzard,*
*As the Arctic unleashes its gale;*
*There's the night falling gray at the end of the day,*
*And there's Death riding hard on their Trail.*
*Man's pluck, and the strength of a dog team—*
*"On, Togo! We trust to your pace."*
*There's the flash of a light—*
*then there's Candle in sight—*
*And Seppala beats Death in the Race!*

## SICK CHILDREN

The city of Nome was in an uproar on the Christmas of my twelfth year. Children were getting sick. Three of them had already died. The name of the sickness they had was diphtheria. Even though I knew dogs couldn't catch it, the word sent a shiver through me. That's because folks were afraid of what the disease could do. And when people are afraid, dogs share their fears.

The Nome commissioner of health came to Sepp to ask for his help. "These sick kids need a special medicine—a serum. The serum can be carried from Anchorage as far as Nenana by train. Then it will have to be carried by dogsled for the rest of the way. We want you to meet another musher at the halfway point from Nenana and bring the serum back here."

"When do you need me to leave?" Sepp asked.

"Soon. Some bigmouthed newspaper reporter thinks a pilot can fly the serum in by plane. I think that's a crackpot idea. No plane has ever made the flight, let alone in the dead of winter. But we have to give these flyboys a chance. If their plan doesn't work, I need you ready to make the run. Sooner or later, folks will come to their senses and realize the only surefire way to carry the serum is by dogsled."

"Thank you for placing your faith in us," Sepp said. "We will not disappoint you."

"I know it," said the commissioner. "Be ready to go at a moment's notice."

In the days after the meeting with the commissioner, Sepp took us on short runs to deliver the mail. But we never went far. Sepp wanted to be near home when the call from the commissioner came through.

Whenever the telephone rang, Sepp leapt up to answer it. He was so jumpy he had us all stirred up. It got so that whenever the phone rang, we'd lift our heads and start baying right along with the bell. We knew what the ringing sound meant. It meant, *This is it, team—mush!*

We'd wait for Sepp to come out of the house and hook us up to the sled. When he didn't, we'd settle back down. All of us were on edge. There were more of us than Sepp would need for the run. We knew he couldn't take all of us, but no dog wanted to be left out.

Then one day the telephone rang, and moments later, Sepp came banging out of the house, dressed for the trail. The time had finally come. We frisked and leapt in the air.

*We're ready to go!* we all said in a chorus of yodels and yips.

"That is right, team! We are off to Nenana to pick up the serum!"

We lifted our heads and howled.

"We are going to help bring that serum back to Nome and cure the sick children!"

We all settled down and were on our best behavior. Polite as you please, we lined up before him and sat. I raised my paw, and a couple of the others copied me. It was okay with me. I considered it a compliment. Everybody was whimpering, *Take me with you, Sepp! Please? Please? Please?*

"I am sorry, boys and girls. I cannot take all of you," Sepp said sadly.

He walked among us and chose twenty of the strongest, fastest dogs. Once Sepp had the serum,

he planned to run with a team of eight. As he explained to Ole, "I will drop some dogs at roadhouses along the way so there will be fresh dogs to replace the tired ones."

He left a team of slow freight dogs behind in the kennel, including Fox, the lead freight dog.

Another dog he left behind was Balto. We didn't know it then, but those same dogs would be called upon by another driver to make the final leg of the run, the one that would deliver the serum to Nome.

As our team of twenty trotted down Nome's Front Street, the whole town turned out to cheer us on our way. Some of these people were the parents of sick children.

"Please hurry back with the serum," they said, their eyes pleading and bright with tears. How could we give them anything but our best?

We headed east along the well-traveled trail, past White Mountain, toward Golovin. We made good time the first day and even better time the second day, dropping dogs at roadhouses along the way. We passed two schools. Sepp stopped at each one. He told the teachers to close the school and to keep the children home and away from anyone passing through from Nome. He was afraid more children would catch diphtheria.

The weather was good, and the trails were hard and fast, the very best kind. We arrived at Isaac's Point, where we bedded down for the night with the family who ran the roadhouse. Sepp dropped off the last two dogs. Now we were down to eight.

"We have covered one hundred thirty miles since leaving Nome," Sepp said to the father. That was nothing to us. We were used to traveling great distances. Any other team that traveled thirty to forty miles a day would have thought they were doing great. Sepp sometimes drove us a hundred miles a day. He asked a whole lot of us and we gave it. But I had a funny feeling that the old man was about to ask more of us than he ever had before. I hoped we could give it to him.

The next morning, we headed for Shaktoolik (shak-TOO-lick), a village on Norton Sound. We arrived at the sound late in the day. The water was iced over and smooth.

"The ice looks pretty good, eh, Togo?" Sepp asked.

I let out a lusty yip. *The ice looks great, Sepp!*

I ran across the frozen bay with my feet churning and my head held high. The ice was hard and dark and strong enough to hold our weight. The wind was at our backs, pushing us forward. We moved across the ice the best way I knew: in a clean, straight line. We had just seen the lights of the Shaktoolik roadhouse on the distant shore when I smelled something mighty familiar. I heard loud barking somewhere ahead. I sped up to see what the hoopla was about.

It was another dogsled team. The first two pairs of dogs were squabbling. For a moment, I thought Sepp was going to stop and help the driver break up the fight, but he didn't. He knew what I knew: that fighting dogs were the musher's own business. Besides, we were on an important errand. We skirted them and kept on our way toward the roadhouse. Then we heard the driver shouting. The wind carried scraps of his voice toward us.

"It's lucky I ran into you! I've got the serum!"

*Serum.* There was that word again.

Sepp put on the brakes, but they wouldn't grip on the slick ice. We went skidding. Sepp shouted, "Gee, Togo!"

I tried to turn right, but the other dogs kept charging ahead. They slammed into my back and pushed me forward. When I got to a patch of rough snow that had blown across the ice, I dug in my claws and slowed us down long enough to haul us around to the right. Now we were headed back the way we had come, toward the other sled.

When we got there, the rumble had broken out in full force, but the musher wasn't paying it any mind. Sepp kept a safe distance. The musher threw Sepp a package wrapped in fur.

Sepp caught it. "Is this the serum?" he hollered.

The musher nodded. "Yes! There's been a change of plan. Five more children have died, so the governor ordered eighteen additional sled teams to join the relay. You'll carry the serum back to Golovin. At Golovin, a fresh driver and team are waiting to carry it along the next leg!"

"I guess we had better get going, then" was all Sepp said. If Sepp was disappointed that we weren't making a longer run, he didn't let on. He was ready to put this new plan into action and give it his all. So was I.

But some of the dogs on our team had other ideas. They wanted to stay and join the rumble. They strained at their harnesses, gnashing their teeth and snarling as they fell in with the brawlers.

"Cut it out!" Sepp yelled at them. He stepped

between the snarling dogs and hauled them back toward the sled. "Children need medicine, and you take time for dogfights?"

The dogs hung their heads. *We're sorry, Sepp!* they whined.

I might not have whined, but I must admit, the thought of crossing Norton Sound all over again made my tongue turn to jerky and my toes curl.

It was bad enough that the wind was now in our faces. But the wind had whipped itself up into a genuine gale-force tizzy.

Our muzzles frosted up as, heads down, we clawed our way back across the bay ice. As we moved into the teeth of the wind, the temperature dropped. Our paw pads set to burning with the cold, and then they went numb. But we knew that there was no stopping. To stop was to die. I felt the sea heaving beneath the ice. All around us, big pieces were breaking up in the swells. If we wound up on a loose piece, we could easily float out to sea—serum and all—and never be seen again. Sepp knew this as well as I did, so he drove us forward like we were in the most important race of our lives. Only now we weren't running for any silver cups. We were running to save lives, including our very own.

Finally, we reached Isaac's Point. The roadhouse was an igloo, a shack made of ice, snow, driftwood, and tundra moss. We dogs were cold and wild with hunger. After unhooking us and leading us into the kennel, Sepp disappeared into the igloo. We could smell our chow cooking—salmon and whale blubber—and we licked our chops.

The kennel was as crude as the igloo, but we'd been there before and I had always liked it. It was close and dark and it smelled like all the sled dogs that had ever stayed there, including me. We had worked hard, crossing Norton Sound twice in one run, and we had earned some rest. After we had gobbled down our chow, most of us dropped to sleep. But I stayed awake to keep an eye on Sepp. I could see out the kennel door that he was still awake and moving around. What was he up to? I watched as he went to the sled and unwrapped the furry package from his bedroll.

"Our instructions are to warm up the serum at every roadhouse. If the medicine freezes, it might not work when we get it to Nome," he said to the Eskimo who owned the igloo.

Finally, my eyelids grew heavy, and I drifted off to sleep. While I slept, my legs moved rapidly as if I were still running across the ice. Suddenly, the line twisted around my neck and the sled slid off the ice into the frozen water. We were sinking into darkness! I woke up with a terrified yip. I sat up and looked around, panting. The other dogs were snoring away. Whew! It was just a dream. A working dog's dream.

I flopped down, faint with relief. I was just settling back to sleep when Sepp came into the kennel. At first, I thought I was dreaming. Then I smelled him as he knelt down and shook me roughly awake. He was bundled up in his parka and ready to head out. He clapped his furry mittens together and shouted to the others, "Time to line up again, boys and girls!"

I lifted my head from my paws. *Already?* I sighed. Outside, the wind howled like a pack of hungry wolves.

"Remember I told you we would be traveling day and night?" Sepp said. "I know you dogs are tuckered out, but there are sick children who need this serum, and we have to get it to them."

I lumbered to my feet. My bones creaked from weariness and cold. *You heard him, brothers and sisters,* I said to the team. *Back to work!*

Outside in the snow, Sepp had the lines and harnesses already laid out. Without any dillydallying, we lined up in our places. Sepp came around and hooked us up: wheel dogs, swing dogs, team dogs, and lead dogs. Fritz was sharing the lead with me. He was almost as good as I was. And he would have to be, to make this run.

As we were pulling away from the roadhouse into the dark and the snow, our host came out and said to Sepp, "Ice no good."

Sepp nodded grimly.

As soon as I saw the bay, I knew what our host meant. During the night, the gale-force winds had busted up the ice into cakes. They were bobbing and creaking out on the water.

The shore was covered with big, jagged rocks,

so we couldn't go that way. And if we moved too far inland, we would lose a day getting to the next relay station. I knew there was only one choice.

Sepp knew it, too. "I guess we will have to travel on the shore ice. What do you say, Togo?"

My tail stuck straight up. I growled in agreement. I led us out onto the narrow strip of solid ice that hugged the shoreline. It was bumpy where the waves had frozen. The sled jostled and rattled around. Sepp got out and ran along next to us. Having only two legs, he slipped and fell often, but each time he got up and kept going.

It was bitterly cold. Big cracks opened in the ice before me. I swerved to go around them. I dodged the places where the ice had splintered into shards as sharp as glass. Meanwhile, the wind knew no mercy. It blew ice shards and sand and sea spray into our eyes. I could barely see where I was going. The dogs were grimly silent, but I could smell their fear. I had to drag them along behind me. My paw pads ached. My harness chafed. My breath came in painful gusts. In extreme cold like that, a dog's lungs could frost over. A dog with frosted lungs was a goner. With an effort, I kept my mouth partly closed as I huffed along.

When I looked over and saw that the beach was clear of boulders, my heart gladdened. I led us off the ice and onto the shore. Sepp called a halt.

*What now, old man?* I growled. That's when I saw that the entire team—me included—was covered in frost. Sepp came down the line, brushing off our coats and bellies. He held our paws in his bare hands and rubbed them. He put salve on our cuts. He risked frostbite to take care of us.

"The last leg will be the toughest," Sepp said.

For eight miles, the shore path went up hills and down dales. Then we found ourselves at the foot of a mountain.

Sepp gazed up toward the peak, which was lost in the clouds. "There is no way around it. We have got to climb this mountain."

The team yowled in protest and sat down hard.

"I know you boys and girls are tired," Sepp said. "I know you have covered two hundred sixty miles in four and a half days. Still, I am asking you to give me one last effort. Can you do it?"

I looked around at the team. With their heads drooping and their tongues hanging out, they were a sorry sight. I knew how they felt. I was beyond exhausted myself. But if they thought I was giving up, they'd never take another step. I leapt in the air and gave a little yelp to show them I was still plenty frisky. *You heard him, brothers and sisters!* I called out. Then I circled around on my long lead and nipped at the flanks of every dog within reach.

*Okay, Chief! Okay! We got it! We'll go!*

*You bet your little rat tails we will,* I said. I got

back in front and pulled the line taut. The dogs looked lively and picked up the slack. They followed me up the side of the icy mountain.

Sepp cracked the whip over our heads. I guess he felt it was making a difference. But it wasn't. It was only turning my brothers and sisters surly and sullen. I let him do it a few more times. Then I stopped and gave him an ornery look. *Enough with the whip, old man. We know what we have to do. And cracking that thing won't make us go any faster.*

Sepp lowered the whip. I turned around and continued trudging up the mountainside.

When we got to the top, I paused to catch my breath and look around. I could just barely make out the roadhouse at Golovin in the distance. We were nearly there.

## THE BALTO BUSINESS

That afternoon, with our last burst of energy, we whipped into Golovin—the final stop for us on the relay. The next driver was waiting for Sepp to hand off the serum. His fresh team was tugging at the harness, raring to go.

Sepp growled at the driver, "You will have to wait, Charlie. Our instructions are to heat up the serum at every roadhouse."

Sepp unhooked us from the sled and took us out of harness. We keeled over in the snow. He unwrapped the serum from his bedroll and staggered into the roadhouse. We lay where we had fallen, too tired to move a hair.

The other team's lead dog took one look at us and said, *That bad, eh?*

*It was worse than that,* I told him. *But you'll have an easier time of it. We took on the worst of it, because we're the best.*

After a bit, Sepp came out of the roadhouse and handed the warmed serum to the driver.

"Good luck!" Sepp called out.

The driver cracked his whip, and the team took off.

Those were the last words I heard as I sank into the deepest, darkest pit of sleep that had ever claimed me. Toward evening, I stirred and lifted my head. My nose twitched. What was that delightful smell?

*Reindeer!*

I sat up and sniffed some more. A herd of reindeer! Suddenly, I forgot all about my aches and pains. I leapt to my feet and shook off the snow.

*I don't know about you kids, but I'm going to chase me some reindeer!*

Big Mary ran to catch up with me, yipping all the way.

I heard Sepp hollering at us, "Get back here, you two!"

But I wasn't going back. I was off duty now, out of harness, and under no obligation to anybody. After all the miles I'd run to carry that serum closer to those sick kids, I figured I'd earned the right to a little fun.

Big Mary and I stayed out in the wilderness for days and had ourselves a fine time. We caught up with the reindeer and chased them far into the Great Forest. We snagged rabbits to eat and some nice tasty birds. We rolled in the snow and in Dead

Things. It felt grand to be off the line and running free.

When the two of us came straggling into Nome a week or so later, the town was still celebrating the delivery of the serum. Word was that the sick children were already getting better. We also saw lots of strangers with cameras. You could have knocked me over with a seagull feather when a stray dog in town told me that Sepp's scrub freight team had run the final leg. A fellow named Kaasen had driven them. But the real kicker was that the lead dog had been Balto! Balto couldn't lead a pack of fleas up a malamute's leg.

I headed home to Little Creek. But little did I know that this was only the beginning of what Sepp would come to call the Balto Business.

Sepp gave me a one-man hero's welcome. He flung me over his shoulder, spun around, and did a little jig. Then he set me back down for the biggest

Man-Dog Hug any mutt had ever gotten.

"You were gone so long, I thought you had been shot by a hunter!" he said. "Oh, Togo, the things you have missed! These reporters are saying Balto is the hero of the Serum Run. I told them *you* were the hero. That you had run five times farther than any dog in the relay. But they will not listen to me. Everybody is talking about Balto, and do you know why? The reporters have taken *your* brilliant track record and given it to *him*! They say Balto's the greatest racing dog in Alaska! But Balto never even ran one single race!"

Poor Sepp. He was all worked up. But for once, I didn't share his beef. The truth was, I didn't care. I was just glad to be home.

We went back to work hauling freight. I found that I got tired more easily than I used to. I guess the Serum Run had wrung me out. Sepp tried hard to put the Balto Business out of his head, but still it bothered him. Balto and his driver had traveled down to the Lower Forty-Eight on a Hero's Tour. In towns all across America, people gathered to celebrate Balto. Balto even went to a place called Hollywood, where they made him a movie star, whatever that is.

News of all this happy hoopla gave Sepp an idea. He packed his bags and took forty-four of us onto a steamship out of Nome. The steamship smelled like gas and garbage. It chugged across the sea to a place in the States called Seattle. A crowd of people cheered us at the dock. There was no snow there, so Sepp hitched us up to a cart and we rode through the streets. Sepp smiled and waved. My man was never happier than when he was in front of an audience, fooling around.

Audiences seemed to like him, too. And us. Wherever we went, crowds gathered to gawk. People snapped pictures of us with their flashing cameras. Sepp would grin and tell them stories about racing and rescues. When he was really excited, he would do handsprings and cartwheels and flips. He was like some two-legged dog doing tricks. In three days, we traveled to more cities than I could keep track of. Wherever we went, Sepp pointed to me and said, "This here is the real hero of the Serum Run."

*Ho-hum.* Did it really matter? What mattered was that the serum had been delivered and the children had gotten better. As for me, I missed the trail. I missed the cold. I missed the wilderness up north. There were too many people here kicking up too much of a fuss. And there wasn't nearly enough snow.

So you can imagine how happy I was when Sepp told us our traveling days were almost over. After we got to New York City and I got my medal from Amundsen, we went north to a place called

Maine. There was snow there, and I guess Sepp missed the snow as much as I did. He had heard tell of folks in Maine who fancied themselves pretty mean dogsled racers.

Hunkered down in the baggage car headed north, Sepp told us about a dog freighter from Alaska who had up and moved to Maine. "He has bred these newfangled sled dogs called Chinooks. He claims they are unbeatable. We will see about that, won't we, boys and girls?"

Sepp took us to a place called Poland Spring, where we entered a big-deal race. A whole passel of folks came to see the Siberians from Alaska race against the Chinooks of Maine. As we gathered at the starting line, someone in the crowd pointed to us and asked, "What kind of dogs *are* those?"

"These are Siberian huskies," Sepp told him proudly. "They are unbeatable."

"Unbeatable? Aren't they awfully *small* to race?"

another asked. "Why, they're the size of wood-chucks!"

"Who said bigger is faster? As you can see from looking at me," Sepp added with a wink, "some-times good things come in small packages."

I eyeballed the dogs in the team lined up next to ours. *What kind of dogs are you?* I asked the lead dog. He was big and shaggy, with loose jowls that would have frozen solid up north.

*We're Chinooks,* the dog said proudly. *We're a cross between Alaskan husky, Saint Bernard, Belgian sheepdog, and German shepherd.*

*You call that a breed?* I snuffed. *I call that Doggie Stew.*

*Our breeder says we're the fastest sled dogs going.*

*Maybe you are and maybe you aren't,* I said. *Then again, what do I know? I'm just a little plume-tailed rat from Little Creek.*

Sepp called out to us, "Okay, boys and girls,

let us show these folks how we do things up in Alaska!"

There was a lady driver on the other side of us. She also had a team of Chinooks. She raised a hand to Sepp and called out, "Good luck, Leonhard!"

"Good luck, Elizabeth!" Sepp called back.

When the gun went off, we started running. I kept the gang line so taut it hummed. The track ran through deep woods. The trail was unfamiliar, but I smelled the strange dogs who had run it before and I followed their scent. It was colder here than in New York City, but compared to Alaska, it was balmy. There was no frost buildup on our fur, no icy-hot feet, no scorched lungs. This would be an easy run. Along the way, we came upon a driver with his sled dogs in a terrible snarl.

"Whoa!" Sepp called out to us as he put on the brakes.

I guess Sepp felt sorry for the musher. We

waited while he helped the driver untangle his dogs. When he had gotten the dogs sorted out, Sepp stepped back on the sled and clucked, urging us back into the race. Even after stopping to help the other team, we broke through the finish tape long before any of the other teams.

So much for Chinooks!

We Siberians took Maine by storm. We went on to win race after race across the state. The lady driver, Elizabeth, was so impressed with our performance that she offered to buy all forty-four of us from Sepp. That worried me until I realized that Sepp was planning to stay put in Poland Spring. I reckoned Constance could do without him for a spell. And I guess Maine was enough like Alaska to make him feel almost at home. He and Elizabeth got together and set up the first breeding kennel in the States for Siberian huskies.

I was fourteen years old by the time the kennel

was up and running. My bones were tired and my eyes weren't working so well. But I wasn't too old or blind to do my bit and sire a whole bunch of Siberian huskies! Siberians became all the rage in the Lower Forty-Eight. Odds are that a Siberian husky you meet today has my blood, or the blood of one of my teammates, running in its veins.

I still heard news about Balto now and then. Sepp told us that he and his teammates had finished their Hero Tour and been sold off to a two-bit showman. They were the sideshow attraction in a traveling carnival. I was sorry to learn that they were poorly fed, never brushed, and hardly ever let out to run. Those dogs may have been bogus heroes, but no one deserved to be treated like that. A man who went to see their cornball act took pity on the dogs and raised money to buy them. He brought them to Ohio, where they lived out their lives in the Cleveland Zoo. Dogs as zoo animals? On the whole, I think I got the better deal.

Sepp liked Maine, but he missed his mate. The day came when Sepp said, "It is time for me to go back to Alaska, Togo."

I raised my front paw and let out a soft woo. *I'm ready to go when you are, old man.*

Sepp sighed and wiped his damp eyes on his sleeve. Sepp was tough stuff, but I could tell this was very hard for him. It was hard for me, too. "Togo, I would love to take you with me, but I do not think you would survive the trip."

I rested my paw on Sepp's knee. *That's okay. I understand.* I knew that I was old, and finished as a sled dog. I had given almost everything I had to the Serum Run. And now I didn't have much left to give.

"You have worked hard all your life, Togo. Stay here with Elizabeth and take it easy. You have earned the rest."

And that's how it happened that Sepp returned to the north and I stayed in Maine. I didn't have it half bad. I lay by the fire in Elizabeth's grand parlor in Poland Spring. I slept almost all the time and I dreamed. I dreamed of racing through the Alaskan wilderness with the wind at my back and the runners cutting deep lines in the snow. Sure, Sepp was gone, but I knew in my bones that sooner or later the old man would come back for me. And when he did, I would be ready to go with him wherever he wanted me to break trail.

# APPENDIX

## More About the Siberian Husky

### Early Days

About 3,000 years ago, the Chukchi (CHOOK-chee) people of Siberia used dogs to pull sleds long distances. The Chukchi valued these dogs for their focus, endurance, and intelligence. The dogs hauled sleds from inland communities to the sea, where the Chukchi hunted whales and seals.

In 1908, a fur trader brought the first of these dogs, now called Siberian huskies, to Alaska to use as sled dogs. There were already sled dogs in Alaska—the much larger Alaskan huskies. The word *husky* comes from *Esky,* a shortened form of the word *Eskimo,* the name then used for the native Alaskans. The natives had worked with sled dogs for hundreds of years. In the snow and ice of Alaska, sled dogs were the most reliable form of transportation between villages and trading outposts. Sled dog racing was—and still is—the most popular sport in Alaska.

Siberian huskies raced for the first time in 1909 in the All Alaska Sweepstakes, a four-day, 408-mile race from Nome to Candle and back again. Siberians proved to be faster than their Alaskan husky and malamute competitors. Later that same year, a sportsman named Charles Ramsay imported a large number of Siberians for racing. His musher, John "Iron Man" Johnson, went on to win the All Alaska in 1910 with a team of Ramsay's Siberians. Wins like this made the breed increasingly popular. Both Roald Amundsen and Robert Peary, in their historic races to reach the North and South

Poles, counted on Siberians to take them to these remotest of destinations.

## Leonhard Seppala and Togo

From 1913 to 1925, Siberians bred and trained by Leonhard Seppala won most of the big races in Alaska. Seppala was no stranger to extreme cold and snow. He was born in Norway, not far from the Arctic Circle. As a young man, in 1900, he came to Nome to work for the Pioneer Mining Company during the height of Alaska's largest gold rush. He became superintendent, in charge of maintaining the water ditches, and drove dogsleds to carry freight and passengers until the mining company was sold in 1923.

In 1925, a deadly diphtheria epidemic broke out in the far northern Alaskan city of Nome. The

Alaskan ports were iced in, so the serum needed to treat the disease could not be delivered by ship. It had to travel by train from the United States to Nenana, the last railroad stop in Alaska.

Getting the serum from Nenana to Nome would be a daunting task. Alaska was in the middle of the coldest winter in twenty years. And the trail from Nenana to Nome was a six-hundred-mile slog through some of the roughest terrain in the territory. It was a route that usually took mail carriers a month to travel. Newspaper stories in the United States—known to Alaskans as the Lower Forty-Eight—had been following the crisis in the north with avid interest. Sick children, miracle serums, extreme weather, and wild terrain: it had all the elements of a gripping story, and it captured the hearts and minds of Americans from coast to coast. Making the story even more dramatic was the raging debate about how to get the serum to the doctor in Nome: by air or by dogsled?

Some people, like William Thompson, the publisher and the editor of the *Fairbanks Daily News-Miner*, thought that dogsleds were old-fashioned and slow. The future of Alaska lay in modern air transport. Airplane was the surest, fastest way to get the serum to Nome. Other people said that airplanes were untested in such icy conditions and that it was impossible to carry enough fuel to make the entire trip. To them, dogsled seemed the best way to go. Scott C. Bone, the territorial governor of Alaska, mulling over his decision until the very last minute, finally decided to go with the dogs.

At a meeting of the Alaska Board of Health, it was agreed that a relay of two fast dogsled teams should carry the serum. One would start from Nenana; the other would start from Nome. They would meet in the middle in Nulato. Then the second musher would double back and carry the serum to Nome. The board members agreed that the best team to make the 630-mile trip from Nome to Nulato and back again was Leonhard Seppala and his legendary lead dog, Togo.

After Seppala had already left Nome for Nulato, five more children died of the disease. In a desperate race against time, Governor Bone ordered U.S. Post Office inspector Edward Wetzler to arrange for an additional eighteen teams to transport the medicine via relays to Nome. Seppala learned of this change of plans only when he met up with musher Henry Ivanoff on the trail from Unalakleet in the midst of a blizzard. Ivanoff handed off the fur-wrapped medicine to Seppala, and Seppala backtracked on the trail toward Shaktoolik, where he handed off the serum to the next musher at Golovin. Even though Seppala was no longer one of only two transporters of the serum, he was still left with the most dangerous leg of the journey, not just one but two trips across the treacherous ice of Norton Sound. His team also ran more miles than any other team in the relay, 169 miles from Nome to Shaktoolik, and an additional 91 miles back to Golovin. Gunnar Kaasen, driving Seppala's scrub freight team with Balto in the lead, made the final 53-mile leg of the journey into Nome.

The citizens of Nome—along with a mob of newspaper reporters—were waiting for the serum to arrive. It seemed as if the whole world was watching when Gunnar Kaasen rode down Front Street and handed over the serum to Dr. Curtis Welcho. Getting the serum to Nome had been a group effort, the work of twenty mushers and teams. But as fate, and the press, would have it, Kaasen and his lead dog, Balto, got all the glory.

When Seppala returned to Nome two days later and found out, he was outraged. Balto was his dog. No one knew better than him that Balto was a simple freight dog. Balto had neither the intelligence, the pluck, nor the racing history of the great Togo. Whether through error or to spice up their story, the reporters took Togo's brilliant record of racing and exploits and gave it to Balto. For the rest of his life, it deeply bothered Seppala that the credit for the Serum Run went to the wrong dog.

Ignorant of this error, the world embraced Balto. Kaasen and his team toured America to great fanfare. They made a short movie, and a bronze statue in Central Park was cast in the likeness of what Seppala insisted was the wrong dog.

In 1926, Seppala followed Kaasen to America, taking with him Togo and forty-three other Siberians. Seppala was a ham who loved performing before crowds. But mostly, he wanted to set the record straight. Togo, the dog who had led his team 260 miles to Balto's 53, was the real hero of the Serum Run.

Seppala ended the tour in Maine, where the team raced against the local sled dogs and beat them soundly. Their victories created a market for Siberians in America. Together with Elizabeth Ricker, heiress to the Poland Spring water fortune, he founded the first American kennel dedicated to breeding and selling Siberian huskies.

Seppala returned to Alaska in 1928, leaving Togo behind. By that time, Togo was nearly blind and could barely walk, and Leonhard feared that his dog, who had traveled so many thousands of miles, would not survive the journey home. A year later, Seppala returned to Poland Spring to say farewell to Togo and to have him put to sleep.

In the end, Seppala succeeded in his mission to tell the story of Togo. When Togo died, the *New York Times Magazine* wrote, "Every once in a while a dog breaks through the daily routine of feeding and barking and tugging at a leash, and for some deed of super-canine heroism, wins the adoring regard of everyone who hears of him." Years later, toward the end of his own life, Seppala would write in his journal, "While my trail has been rough at times, the end of the course seems pretty smooth, with downhill going and a warm roadhouse in sight. And when I come to the end of the trail, I feel that along with my many friends, Togo will be waiting and I know that everything will be all right."

Togo's body was mounted and put on display in the Yale Peabody Museum in New Haven, Connecticut. Later, it was returned to Alaska. The stuffed Togo is still receiving visitors at the Iditarod Trail Headquarters in Wasilla.

For more information about Togo, Balto, and the Serum Run, visit:

- cmnh.org/site/AtTheMuseum/OnExhibit/PermanentExhibits/Balto.aspx

- litsite.org/index.cfm?section=Digital-Archives&page=Land-Sea-Air&cat=Dog-Mushing

  To read more about Leonhard Seppala, try:
- seppalakennels.com/articles/leonhardseppala.htm

# The Iditarod

Today in Alaska, sled dogs no longer play the vitally important role they once did. Trains, trucks, bush planes, and the "iron dog"—or snowmobile—now do the work that mushers and their dogs once did. But thanks to a few visionary Alaskans, the sport of sled dog racing still thrives.

In 1964, an amateur historian from Wasilla named Dorothy Page wanted to celebrate Alaskan history and memorialize the Serum Run. Together with a musher named Joe Redington, she came up with the idea of an annual sled dog race. They organized volunteers to clear the trail and raised funds for a $25,000 winner's cup. In 1967, to commemorate the centennial of Alaska's becoming a U.S. territory, they held a fifty-six-mile sprint from Knik to Big Lake. The race was run for two years before interest waned.

But Joe Redington was not discouraged. He pictured an event that was more challenging. The long-distance race would cut right through the heart of Alaska's rugged wilderness, tracing the old Gold Rush and freight delivery route. With some help from the U.S. Army, volunteers cleared the 1,000-mile trail from Anchorage to Nome. First held in 1973, the event was called the Iditarod, named after the native Alaskan word for the trail. Now held every March, it is touted and trademarked as "the Last Great Race on Earth." The Iditarod celebrates the pioneer spirit of the mushers and their courageous and durable sled dogs, among which Togo will forever stand as a shining example.

To learn more, visit the official site of the Iditarod Sled Dog Race:

- iditarod.com

You might also want to check out:

- alaskacenters.gov/iditarod.cfm

Teachers looking for Iditarod-based curriculum ideas can go to:

- iditarod.com/teachers

## The Siberian Husky Today

Today's Siberians are a medium-sized working breed with a thick coat that consists of two layers: a dense undercoat and a topcoat made up of straight guard hairs. Thanks to their double coats, Siberians can survive temperatures as low as sixty degrees below zero. Contrary to what many people think, Siberians are perfectly comfortable in warmer weather because their outer coat deflects the sun's rays. Siberians' coats come in many colors. The most common combination is black and white, although they can also be copper with brown spots. They have plumed tails, prick ears, and long legs made for running. Their eyes are almond-shaped, either brown or blue. They howl as well as bark. Siberians have been recognized as a breed by the American Kennel Club since 1930.

To find out more about the breed, visit:

- akc.org/breeds/siberian_husky
- shca.org

## Owning a Siberian Husky

Siberians are gentle and intelligent and, if trained early, can make wonderful house pets for all ages. Because they have been bred to pull sleds and to race, they want—and need—to exercise daily.

When taking them out for their daily run, it is best to keep them on a leash. Like Togo, they are gifted escape artists. A loose Siberian will cut and run and be miles away before you can catch it. They also climb fences, tunnel under fences, and jump through windows.

Siberians learn by imitating humans. After watching their masters, they have been known to flip light switches, turn on appliances, and open refrigerator doors so they can help themselves to a snack! Like all highly intelligent creatures, they are easily bored. Your Siberian will be happiest if you take it out to run every day and vary your routine. An even better way to keep a Siberian happy is to train it to pull you on a sled or cart.

A Siberian will keep you busy with the brush and the vacuum cleaner. It sheds its coat (both layers) once a year. The inner coat comes out in big, furry clumps. You will have to brush your Siberian every day, and even then, there will still be husky hair all over your clothes and upholstery. Some people make use of the shed hair. They collect it and spin it into yarn to make beautiful sweaters and hats! But if dog hair bothers you, steer clear of a Siberian!

To learn whether a Siberian husky is the right dog for you, visit:

- shca.org/shcahp2b.htm

For information about adopting a Siberian husky, visit:

- siberianrescue.com

Togo—Leonhard Seppala's lead dog—stands in front of his team after the Serum Run.

Leonhard Seppala and Togo

The Serum Run team. Togo is on the left. Fritz is on the right.

# If you loved Togo, you'll love Dash, too!

## Coming in Summer 2014!

## My name is Dash, and dashing is what I was born and bred to do.

An angry ocean has all but swallowed up the good ship *Mayflower*. For days, it has been lashed by rains and tossed by waves. The deck teeters beneath my feet. I claw my way upward one moment, only to come slipping and sliding down the next. The ship lurches, and I tumble head over tail. I stand up and shake myself hard. I am soaked to the skin. My head reels! This is no life for a simple hunting dog.

With information about Plymouth Colony, the first Thanksgiving, English springer spaniels, and more.